A RIGHT COZY CULINARY CRIME

A RIGHT COZY CRIME

WENDY H. JONES   SHEENA MACLEOD   JEANNE SWARTZ

SANDRA IRELAND   LISA KNUDSEN HARKRADER

MARTI M. MCNAIR   NICOLETTE LEMMON

SHEILA DENE' LAWRENCE   SHANA FROST   DK SNYDER

PAULA BARR

Scott and Lawson Publishing

Print ISBN: 978-1-913372-11-8

eBook ISBN: 978-1-913372-10-1

Dedicated to cozy mystery authors worldwide who inspire me in many ways. May your ideas keep coming and the words keep flowing.

CONTENTS

INTRODUCTION

Despite a supposed economic downturn, reading still seems to be popular worldwide. Within this, crime fiction is strong and the subgenre of Cozy Mystery, stronger still. Readers love books which entertain and where ordinary people stick their nose in and solve the crime with no, or little, help from the police or any other law enforcement agency. This book contains eleven such mysteries which are sure to bring you hours of joy. Sit down with a cup of tea or coffee, or even a glass of wine and savour the delicious stories within its pages.

Please note both British and American English are used in this book. Stories set in the UK use British English. Those in the USA, use American English.

Chapter One

HAGGIS AND HOMICIDE

Sheena Macleod

It's Burns Night, and murder is on the menu at the Loch Tarry Inn. A temperamental chef, a missing sgian dubh and a group of disgruntled guests from the local Historic Poets' Society provide the perfect recipe for murder.

A Scottish Culinary Village Mystery

A loud crash, followed by a piercing shriek, had the landlady of the Loch Tarry Inn racing towards the kitchen. Fiona McGregor pushed open the door and gasped. Never in her life had she seen such utter bedlam. Broken dinner plates littered the floor. Big Archie, the chef, dressed in his whites, sat red-faced on top of the kitchen island, his arms crossed around him. Her mother, Carol, knelt in front of the gas stove with her head in the oven.

'For the love of the wee man,' Fiona bellowed to get their attention.

'Ooh. Fiona,' Carol said as she pulled her head out from the oven and sat back on her hunches. 'You fair gave me a fright, lass.'

'I gave *you* a fright?' Fiona couldn't believe what she was hearing. 'What on earth is going on? And you,' she said to Big Archie. 'Get down from there.'

'I can't,' Archie squeaked. 'There's a mouse in here. I saw it.'

Carol roared with laughter. 'A wee, timorous beastie, was it Big Archie? Well, it fair set a panic in your breastie.'

Fiona's morning had descended into chaos, and it wasn't even ten o'clock. She turned to Carol. 'Mum?'

'Oh, Fiona, calm yersel' doon. I was just having a laugh.' Carol held up a dark-coloured, metal pot scourer. 'I was scrubbing out the oven when the scourer went skidding across the floor. Well, that is, after I *accidentally* kicked it.' She held up the offending object. 'Here's yer mouse, Big Archie.'

Archie slipped down from the kitchen island and tilted his chin in the air. 'I ken what I saw. And it wasn't that thing,' he said, pointing to the scourer. He turned to Fiona and placed a hand on his hip. 'It was a mouse.' Fiona went to speak, but Big Archie held up a hand, palm towards her. 'I'm no' cooking in this kitchen until the wee pest's been caught.'

'Archie. I'm begging you.' Fiona said and glanced towards her mother for support, which wasn't forthcoming. 'It's Burns Night. You've a haggis dinner to cook.'

Big Archie was having none of it. Reason had truly left him.

'I mean it, Fiona, you'll need to get health and safety in to check this place over.'

'Away with you,' Carol said and guffawed. 'Health and Safety for a pot scourer. Aye, they'll love us for that.'

'In case you've both forgotten,' Fiona said and turned to leave, 'we've twelve guests coming tonight. The Historic Poets' Society are expecting a Burns Supper. So, pull yourselves together and stop dithering, or it may very well be the last supper we serve them.'

Catriona hesitated as she pulled the kitchen door closed behind her, leaving them to sort it out between themselves. Field mice often sought shelter in the winter, but she was certain none had come into her kitchen. Regardless, a deep clean was called for. How the staff would find time, in between preparing mountains of tatties, neeps and haggis, she didn't know. But if it got Big Archie back and cooking in the kitchen, she would find a way. 'Mrs Murdoch,' she called and set off in search of the housekeeper.

⁂

The wail of bagpipes set Fiona's teeth on edge. She loved the sound of the pipes as much as the next person, but the incessant noise had been droning on for over an hour. She laid down the tattie peeler and opened the kitchen door leading to the back of the Loch Tarry Inn. 'Alistair,' she yelled, attempting to draw the piper's attention.

Alistair MacIntosh looked over, and she held up a hand. 'Give it a break. What's going on with you?'

'Nerves.' He grimaced. 'I've never piped the chieftain haggis in before.'

'Get over it, laddie. You'll be braw, as always. If you've nothing to do, you can always give me a hand in here, setting out the chairs in the function room.'

Alistair's grin lit his face and set his freckles bouncing. 'That would be grand, Fiona. I need to keep busy, and it's freezing out here.' He sidestepped the chef, who tried to sidle in through the door just as he attempted to enter. Alistair stepped back with a smile. 'On ye' go, Big Archie. After you.'

Big Archie strode into the kitchen and flicked his eyes between the potato peeler in Fiona's hand and Mrs Murdoch's back as she scrubbed the sink with bleach. 'Ooh. There will be nae mice now. Thanks, Mrs M.'

Mrs Murdoch turned and winked at Fiona. 'Ye soft lump o' lard that ye are, Archie. Aye, well, you'll be able to get on now. That's me finished. I'll start setting the tables.'

Big Archie turned to Fiona, a confused look on his face. 'Erm. Where's the ceremonial haggis? Were you no' meant to pick it up?'

Fiona's hand flew to her mouth, and she turned a full circle. 'Noo. I can't believe I forgot to pick up the chieftain haggis. With all that nonsense earlier, I completely forgot. Archie?'

'Don't look at me. Archie turned and picked up a turnip. 'I've got neeps to prepare.'

Fiona pulled off her apron. 'Hold the fort, Archie. I'll no' be long,' she said as she headed out to see Mo MacDougall, owner of the butcher's shop and known around the village as Mo Butcher. She could have sent her mum, but Carol would have spent hours blethering to Mo, who seemed to know all the villagers' secrets even before they did.

Malcolm McNab, Chair of the Historic Poets' Society, was the first to arrive in the hotel foyer, half an hour before the pre-arranged time. Fiona grimaced at the dairy farmer's early arrival, but smiled as she came out from behind the reception desk to greet him. When she'd picked up the haggis, Mo Butcher mentioned that Malcolm was having to sell some of his fields.

Dressed in a Highland outfit complete with McNab tartan

trousers, Malcolm paced the carpet. 'Oh, Fiona. What a rush it was to get here before Kim.' He looked at his watch, 'but I made it.' He glanced out the window. 'And just in time, too,' he said as a blue VW Beetle with the registration plate BU59RNS trundled to a stop in the car park.

The society's secretary, Councillor Kim Mackenzie, hurried into the foyer, clutching a clipboard. She ran a hand through her blonde bobbed hair. 'It's blowing a hoolie out there,' she said, removing a page from the clipboard and thrusting it towards Fiona. 'A copy of the itinerary for tonight's toasts and speeches.' She turned to Malcolm and handed him a copy. 'This will be the best Burns Supper yet.' Kim straightened her tartan shawl and let out a deep, contented sigh. 'The world's watching us, Malcolm. This will put our wee village on the map, just you wait and see.'

Aye, right, Fiona thought. The nearest Kim and the Historic Poets' Society would get to being seen was from the camera overlooking the car park.

Malcolm flicked a finger down the list. 'Oh, Kim. I don't know about putting Iain Campbell's reading before mine. Can you change that?'

As Kim and Malcolm argued over the itinerary, Fiona escorted them through to the lounge. She left them there and returned to the desk. Carol would take care of the drinks: a complimentary dram of whisky for each person on arrival.

Clutching a copy of *Burns' Selected Poems*, Iain Campbell, fruit farmer and treasurer of the society, led the rest of the guests into the foyer. Iain regarded himself as the most skilled in the society at reciting Burns' poetry. Miss Buchanan, a retired English teacher, disagreed. Fiona ignored the petty comments between Iain and Miss Buchanan as she escorted them and the other guests into the lounge.

The last guest to enter the lounge, Reverend James Stewart, headed straight for the bar. Drawn by the sight of Carol holding a bottle of Talisker whisky, he pushed up the round glasses perched on the end of his bulbous nose and waved to get her attention. 'Ooh, thanks, Carol. A wee dram to get the celebrations started.'

&a.

Alistair piped Fiona and the guests through to the function room, his kilt swinging as he skirled the bagpipes as skilfully as any piper had before him. Doctor Gordon, elected host, led the procession in behind Alistair and stood at a chair at the head of the long table. Fiona took the seat beside him.

Once everyone was seated, Doctor Gordon held up a hand. 'Welcome to the Historic Poets' Society's Annual Burns Supper. And thank you, Fiona McGregor and the Loch Tarry Inn, for accommodating us once again. Our chairman, Malcolm McNab, will say a few words about the bard.'

When Malcolm finished his *Immortal Memory* speech, and a toast had been raised to Burns, Doctor Gordon thanked him. 'Now, let us say grace. Some hae meat,' he intoned and then completed the traditional *Selkirk Grace* before sitting down.

Carol placed a bowl of piping hot Scotch broth before each guest. As they tucked into the starter, Fiona lifted her spoon and sighed with relief. So far, so good. Despite the chaotic start to the day, perhaps the evening would be a success after all.

After Carol cleared the last empty soup bowl from the table, the piper entered playing *A Man's a Man for A' That*, followed by the red-faced cook carrying the chieftain haggis on a large silver platter. The guests clapped as Big Archie placed the haggis in front of Doctor Gordon, who stood and held up the Loch Tarry Inn's ancient *sgian dubh*.

'Fair fa' your honest, sonsie face. Great Chieftain o' the puddin' race,' he recited. When he reached the third verse of the *Address to a Haggis*, Doctor Gordon fell silent and mimed sharpening the dagger. He plunged the *sgian dubh* deep into the haggis, splitting the skin from one end to the other as he said,

'His knife see rustic Labour dight. An' cut ye up wi' ready slight.'

Miss Buchanan scoffed as the doctor stuttered his way through the last verse. Fiona joined the chorus of shushes sent in the teacher's direction.

Doctor Gordon completed the traditional address, and glasses clinked around the table. Fiona tilted her whisky glass towards the haggis and joined the toast, '*Slàinte Mhath.*'

Carol placed a plate of haggis, neeps and tatties before Fiona, along with a small jug of whisky sauce, and Fiona nodded her approval. Despite the earlier chaos, the meal looked delicious.

After glasses of cranachan had been served and eaten, Big Archie and Carol brought through the shortbread and coffee, which signified the end of the meal and the start of the toasts and poetry readings.

Constable Angus Fraser raised a toast to the lassies. When he finished, Elspeth Maclean, deputy chair, stood and snorted. 'On behalf of the lassies, thank you, Angus. You did a rare job there.' She glanced around the table and rolled her eyes. 'Like Burns himself, using his wit to woo a' the lassies, whatever next, Angus?' she said to roars of laughter and loud clapping.

When Iain Campbell finished reading *Tam O'Shanter* to a round of applause, Malcolm pursed his lips and crossed his arms. Iain glowered and shook his copy of *Burns' Selected Poems* at their chairperson before sitting down, a thunderous look on his face.

Kim stared over at Iain and shook her head. 'For someone who claims to be our greatest Burns enthusiast, you're doing a grand job of trying to destroy this celebration.'

'There's no '*claims to be*' about it, Kim,' Iain said, his voice rising. 'You ken fine I'm the most skilled amongst us at reciting the bard. I've awards tae prove it. And while we're at it, that alone should entitle me to host our next Burns Supper.'

'O wad some Pow'r the giftie gie us, to see oursels as ithers see us,' Elspeth quoted from her *Pocketbook of Burns' Poetry* and glared at Iain.

Mo Butcher shook her head, 'We're no' going through all this again, Iain.' She flapped her hand. 'Just get on with it, Kim. We've wasted enough time over this.'

Holding up a page from her clipboard, Kim read out the poem, *To A Mouse*. When she finished, Miss Buchanan, who'd muttered throughout the reading, said, 'The wee mouse is cowering, Kim, so you need to pronounce it cow'rin, not coo'ran.'

Kim reddened. 'You're no' in school now, Miss Buchanan, give it a rest.'

Fiona shifted in her seat and nodded to Doctor Gordon, urging him to intervene, but Miss Buchanan hadn't finished with Kim. 'Hmm. If you could recite Burns as well as you can block funding for the village hall, Councillor Mackenzie, I'd be clapping along with the others.'

'Nobody's blocked funding,' Kim replied. 'A planning issue is holding up the process.'

'Ah, yes. Kim. Hopefully, you'll get that sorted soon,' Doctor Gordon said. As well as a Burns enthusiast, he played the accordion. 'It was the musical society, Miss Buchanan, that put the proposal before the council for a matched grant towards the refurbishment of the village hall.'

'Excuse me. I've got to take this call,' Malcolm jumped up from his seat, phone in hand. 'Urgent business,' the chairperson added and headed for the door.

As Reverend Stewart picked up his glass of whisky and stood to make a toast, the guests around the table let out a collective groan.

'Keep it short,' one of the guests called. 'Remember it's no' a sermon you're giving.'

When the reverend finished talking and raised his glass, Iain slumped forward. 'Sorry, I don't feel well. A bit sleepy, and that's nothing to do with your speech, reverend,' he added. 'Likely, I've just had too much to eat and drink.' Iain shuffled out of his seat.

'I'll go and get some fresh air. Carry on without me,' he said and hurried from the room.

Fiona caught Doctor Gordon's attention and pointed to her watch. He nodded his agreement and held up a hand. 'We'll take a ten-minute break.'

The reverend turned to speak to Kim, seated next to him. As he did so, he nudged her arm, sending the contents of her whisky glass over her tartan shawl. 'Sorry, Kim. My arm slipped,' he said and offered her his napkin.

'Leave it be. I'll go and fetch another one,' she muttered as she looked down at her soaked shawl. 'I'll check on Iain while I'm out.'

Constable Fraser tilted his glass in Kim's direction. 'You're no' thinking of driving home for a shawl?'

'No, Constable, I'm just fetching one from my car,' she replied, shaking her head. 'My husband's picking me up later.'

Constable Fraser turned to Elspeth and tilted his head towards the door as Kim left. 'I can't believe Kim cancelled the ceilidh tonight. I was fair looking forward to dancing *The Eightsome Reel*. As deputy chair, could you no' have done something?'

Elspeth frowned. 'We're all disappointed, Constable Fraser, but Kim didn't cancel the ceilidh. There's no need to be so hard on her. The band let her down. Now, shoosh.' she said, and opened her *Pocketbook of Burns' Poetry*. 'It's my turn next to read.'

Fiona waited while glasses were refilled, then checked her watch. Malcolm and Kim still hadn't returned. Likely, they were attending to Iain. She caught Elspeth's attention, pointed to her watch and held up five fingers. Letting the deputy chair know they would resume in five minutes.

Before Elspeth could reply, the lights went out, plunging the diners into darkness. The clatter of seats being pushed back and the hum of conversation filled the room.

Carol hurried in from the kitchen, shining her phone torch in front of her, followed closely by Big Archie. 'Looks like a power cut,' she said in a raised voice to make sure everyone heard.

Fiona helped Carol search the dresser for more candles, while the guests milled around in the semi-darkness. She startled when Constable Fraser appeared beside her. 'Where's the fuse box?' he asked.

Holding her phone torch in front of her, Fiona led Constable Fraser down the hallway. She yanked open the door of a large walk-in cupboard and froze. Iain Campbell lay slumped on the floor with his back against the wall, his copy of *Burns' Selected Poems* by his hand. Liquid dribbled from his mouth, and blood stained the front of his white shirt. Fiona screamed.

❧

Constable Fraser shifted his sporran to one side and hunched down beside Iain. As he pushed the book of poems aside with his pen, a torn piece of paper slipped from the pages. Fiona bent to pick it up, twisting her neck forward to read what was on the page as she did so. 'Don't touch anything,' he said and straightened. He flicked the switch on the fuse box, and the lights came on. 'Looks like something tripped the switch. Fetch Doctor Gordon, Fiona. Oh, and make sure no one leaves. I'll phone this in.'

Fiona stepped into the hallway and was met by a sea of anxious faces. Carol pushed her way to the front. 'Fiona?'

'I'm fine, Mum. Doctor Gordon, you're needed in there. It's Iain Campbell.' Fiona took a deep breath and flapped a hand. 'Okay, everyone else, go back into the function room. Constable Fraser will be through soon. He'll explain everything then.' She rubbed her hands down her face. 'For now, the Loch Tarry Inn's on lockdown. No one's to leave.'

The doctor stepped out from the cupboard and shook his head. 'There was nothing I could do. It looks like Iain's been stabbed.'

Carol shuffled from foot to foot. 'Get Constable Fraser, Fiona.'

'He's already in there, Mum.'

'No, I mean, get him out *here*.' Carol's face paled. 'Our ancient *sgian dubh* is missing.'

Fiona shook her head to clear her thoughts. 'What do you mean, missing?'

'Well, it's no' on the platter wi' the haggis skin where it should be.' Carol nodded towards the kitchen. 'Big Archie's searching for it as we speak. I was on my way to let you know when I heard you scream.' As her mother opened her mouth to continue, Fiona lifted a hand, cutting her off. Carol could develop a conspiracy theory faster than Fiona could say, Loch Ness Monster.

Carol sniffed but remained silent.

'Wait. Let me think,' Fiona said as she paced the hallway. 'When did you last see the *sgian dubh*?'

'Hogmany?'

Fiona groaned. 'Mum. Seriously. I wasn't asking you when we last used it.'

'Ooh, sorry, Fiona. It's the shock. When Big Archie brought the haggis platter back into the kitchen, he laid it to one side as we had to serve the cranachan. It was only when we went back in there with the candles to start clearing up that Big Archie noticed the dagger was missing from the platter. And, now.' Carol flicked her eyes towards the cupboard. 'I'm wondering if our missing *sgian dubh* could have been used to stab Iain Campbell?'

The voices around Fiona faded as Constable Fraser returned to the function room just as Big Archie held up the Loch Tarry's *sgian dubh*. The constable's eyes fixed onto the chef standing there, red-faced and shaking, the bloodied dagger clutched in his hand, his apron smeared with streaks of crimson.

Big Archie's eyes flicked down to the dagger, then back to Constable Fraser. 'The *sgian dubh* was under the table,' he uttered, his voice breaking. 'I picked it up.' He rubbed his hand down his bloodied apron, as if trying to wipe away the evidence of his grim discovery.

Constable Fraser pulled his phone from his sporran and snapped a photo of Big Archie holding the dagger. 'Now, lay the *sgian dubh* down, Archie. There's no need for anyone else to get hurt. We don't want any more bother.'

'Bother,' Archie screeched. He thrust the dagger onto the table. 'There will be nae bother from me. I'm telling you, I found it under the table.'

'Excuse me, Constable Fraser,' the piper hopped from foot to foot, waving his hands, 'Big Archie's telling the truth. I saw him pick the dagger up.'

Constable Fraser shook his head from side to side. 'Aye, well, Alistair, that's as maybe. But who's to say Big Archie didn't put it there in the first place?'

Archie paled. 'I did not.'

'Archie Thomson,' Constable Fraser said as he gripped the chef's arm. 'I'm taking you in for questioning regarding the murder of Iain Campbell. I'll wait here with you until my colleagues get here. The rest of you wait in the lounge. This room is now a crime scene.'

❧

Fiona slid onto a stool in the lounge to talk to Carol, who was drying glasses behind the bar. 'That's the police here. They've taken Big Archie away. There's no way he would have done this, Mum.'

'I agree,' Carol said as she scrunched up the tea towel and

threw it onto the counter. 'Constable Fraser was too hasty in deciding that Big Archie stabbed Iain.'

'Then, we need to find out who did, before Archie's arrested. What have we got?'

'Well. Could Iain have been poisoned to get him to leave the function room? He didn't look well before he left.'

'Our food was fine,' Fiona said. 'No one else has felt sick. Have they?'

'No. And of course, Iain wasn't poisoned,' Carol agreed. 'Which makes me wonder, could someone have sedated him? He did say he felt sleepy.'

Fiona noticed Reverend Stewart standing at the side of the room, clutching a hip flask. 'Hold on,' she said to Carol. 'Reverend,' she called and waved him over to the bar.

'Ooh, no thanks, Fiona,' he said as he arrived beside them. 'I'll not bother with another dram, I think I've had enough.'

'I wasn't offering you a whisky. Constable Fraser made it clear there's to be no alcohol consumed until everyone has given their statements to the police. What are you doing with that hip flask? You're no' going against police orders, are you?'

'Me. Absolutely, not,' he replied, glancing around as if looking for an escape route.

'So, what's in there?' Fiona asked, pointing to the pewter flask.

He unscrewed the cap and passed it over. Fiona sniffed the contents. 'Smells suspiciously like coffee.'

Reverend Stewart held up his hands in surrender. 'That's because it is. Erm. And cocoa, whisky and condensed milk. Flavoured with a wee spot of vanilla essence. It's my Scottish cream liqueur recipe.'

'So, what are you doing with it in your flask?' Fiona asked.

He held a hand to his mouth and coughed. 'It was for the cranachan.'

Carol frowned. 'What do you mean?'

'Don't tell Big Archie.' He flushed a deep scarlet. 'I brought it to give the pudding a wee bit more flavour. Archie never puts in enough whisky.'

Fiona groaned in exasperation. They were getting nowhere. 'Did you notice anything at all unusual tonight?' Fiona asked him, desperate for something to go on.

'What's said to me in confidence stays in confidence,' Reverend Stewart said and pushed his glasses up onto the bridge of his nose.

'Come on, reverend,' Carol said. 'Big Archie's freedom's at stake here.'

'All I'll say is someone in the society is no' playing fair about the village hall,' he said and walked away.

Needing time to think, Fiona made herself a flat white on the coffee machine behind the bar. 'That was a rather cryptic reply, wasn't it?' she said to Carol and screwed up her face in concentration as the drink spluttered into the cup. 'What member of the society?'

'Could the reverend have been referring to the funds the society raised towards the village hall refurbishment?' Carol asked. 'Iain Campbell was their treasurer. Had he found something out?'

Fiona sipped her coffee and looked around the lounge at the guests, whispering together in small clusters. Kim sat at a table, talking to Miss Buchanan and Elspeth. 'We should speak to Kim. When she left to get her shawl, she said she'd check on Iain. Come on, let's see what Councillor Mackenzie's got to say.'

'Hmph,' Miss Buchanan uttered as Fiona and Carol joined the table. The teacher folded her arms and tilted her head towards Kim. 'The villagers have been raising funds for years towards the refurbishment of the village hall, and now you're saying the matched council grant is no' happening.'

'Like I said earlier,' Kim replied, 'a planning issue is holding things up at the council end. Hopefully, we'll hear soon that the issue has been resolved. Until then, there's not a lot I can do.'

Carol leant forward and lowered her voice. 'When you spilt

the whisky, Kim, you went out to get another shawl. Did you see Iain?'

'No. And I didn't see Malcolm either. I assumed he was with Iain.'

'And was he?' Miss Buchanan asked.

'I told you I didn't see either of them.'

Fiona nodded. 'When did you come back into the function room, Kim?'

'I got back just as the lights went out.'

'What about Malcolm?' Carol added and looked around the table. 'He said he had to take an urgent phone call. Did he return before the lights went off?'

'Definitely not,' Fiona said. 'I noticed because I was watching for Kim and Malcolm to return so Elspeth could start her reading.'

Elspeth nodded. 'Malcolm returned not long after Kim,' she said. 'Just before you and Big Archie came through, Carol.'

'That was a long phone call,' Carol said and raised her eyebrows at Fiona.

Fiona and Carol left them arguing about the funding for the village hall and set off to speak to Malcolm. As they made their way there, they were stopped by Mo Butcher, who ushered them aside. 'When you found Iain, Fiona, did he have a letter on him?' she asked, almost in a whisper. 'It would have been in his book of poems.'

Recalling the book beside Iain, Fiona paused. 'Part of a letter with Housebricks and Ian Campbell's name on it fell out when Constable Fraser moved the book.'

Mo Butcher nodded. 'That's Housebricks Land Development and Construction Company. It's a private housing developer. I received a letter from them, too. That's not unusual. The farmers in the village are always getting letters from developers asking if we'll sell some fields.' She glanced around and licked her lips. 'Housebricks Land Development and Construction Company intend to build luxury holiday lets in the village.

Unlike someone else, I refused to consider selling any of my fields to them.'

Interesting, Fiona thought. When she'd picked up the haggis, Mo mentioned that Malcolm needed to sell off some of the fields from his dairy farm. No wonder he'd looked anxious when he arrived. The village gossip would soon be abuzz with the news. 'You mean Malcolm McNab?'

'Aye. That's exactly who I mean,' Mo Butcher said and made to move away. 'Ask him.'

Fiona and Carol returned to the bar. Sitting alone at the counter, Fiona thought through everything they'd found out. Housebricks Land Development and Construction Company wanted to build luxury holiday lets in the village. A planning application for this would have been submitted to the council for approval. Kim mentioned that a planning issue was holding up the release of the matched grant for the refurbishment of the village hall. What planning issue? Part of a letter from the development company addressed to Iain had fallen from the book he had on him. Malcolm intended to sell some of his fields. Everything seemed to come back to the development company and the village hall. The last piece of the jigsaw fell into place for Fiona. Malcolm's great-grandfather had given the land for the village hall to be built on.

Fiona turned to Carol, who was stacking glasses behind the bar, 'Gather everyone together.' She hoped for Big Archie's sake that she was right.

'During the Burns Supper tonight,' Fiona said and nodded to Councillor Kim Mackenzie, 'Iain intended to reveal that if the council approved the planning application for a new private housing development to be built on Malcolm's land, it would mean the loss of the village hall. Part of a letter from the developers, Housebricks Land Development and Construction Company, to Iain, was in the book he had on him.'

Fiona turned her attention to Mo Butcher, who nodded. 'When Iain showed that letter to Mo Butcher yesterday, he pointed out something to her about one of the fields Malcolm intended to sell. The sale included Cowslip Meadow.'

'Malcolm's great-grandfather gave Cowslip Meadow for the village hall to be built on,' Mo Butcher said.

A gasp went around the room, and Fiona held up a hand. 'Iain wrote to the developers about this, only to receive a reply informing him that no legal papers had been drawn up to support any donation of Cowslip Meadow to the village.'

'I warned Iain not to confront Malcolm about this tonight,' Mo Butcher added.

Malcolm held up a hand. 'Let me speak. As you all know, my dairy farm's being run into the ground. Each year, it costs more to maintain it than I can make. When the letter from the developers came in offering to buy six of my fields, I couldn't refuse. It was only when I saw the deeds that I realised the land included the field my great-grandfather gave to build the village hall on. The developers refused to buy from me if that field wasn't included. I had no choice but to consider selling Cowslip Meadow to them. I was desperate.'

'And, Iain Campbell?' Fiona asked.

'Iain followed me out so he could speak to me alone. He was furious about the possible loss of the village hall. We argued. The letter from the developers about Cowslip Meadow must have ripped as I pulled it from his book. I didn't mean to stab Iain, but I couldn't let him read that letter out.'

In the function room, Fiona closed the ornate wooden box the ancient *sgian dubh* would be placed in once it was returned from the police station. The dagger had been in her family for generations and was as much a part of the Craig Tarry Inn as the foundation stones it was built on. Fiona gently lifted the box sans *sgian dubh* into the back of the large dresser and locked the door. The police would hopefully return the family heirloom before it needed to be brought out again at Hogmanay.

The officers who'd been in the function room had arrested Malcolm McNab and removed him to the police station. Malcolm had lifted the dagger from the platter in the kitchen and hidden it under the table on his return to the function room, having cleaned himself up and switched off the lights at the fuse box to cover his actions. As he'd been escorted out the Loch Tarry Inn, Malcolm promised to transfer ownership of Cowslip Meadow to the village. Fiona was certain Reverend Stewart was to thank for that. But, whatever it was he'd whispered to Malcolm would remain a mystery.

Big Archie finally returned with Constable Fraser. 'Oh, Carol,' Archie said as he bounded through the door of the function room and hurried towards her. 'It's grand to be back. I've had plenty time to think things over. You were right.'

'Aye?' Carol said. 'And, what was I right about?'

'It was a pot scourer I saw in the kitchen this morning, no' a wee mouse. But don't be scaring me like that again.'

Their conversation was interrupted when Doctor Gordon came in with his accordion and sat on one of the chairs. 'My wife brought it.'

The guests set to with gusto, scraping back tables and chairs to make room for the dancing.

'Take your partners,' Doctor Gordon called as he played the opening notes of *The Dashing White Sergeant*.

Mrs Gordon grabbed Constable Fraser's hand and pulled him onto the dance floor. 'Oh, aye, count me in,' he said and grinned.

When the clock struck midnight, the guests formed a circle and held hands. Fiona, Carol and Big Archie shuffled into place between them. *For Auld Lang Syne*, the revellers sang. Big Archie's voice soared above the others. Let him have his moment, Fiona thought. Not even Miss Buchanan complained. The pot of stovies the chef had made to finish the night off may well have played a part in the teacher's silence. Fiona McGregor smiled. What would she do without Big Archie?

BIO:

Sheena Macleod is a published historical fiction author and a prize-winning and published short story writer. She lives in a seaside town on the East Coast of Scotland. You can find her online at https://www.sheenas-books.co.uk

RECIPES

Cranachan

Cranachan is a traditional Scottish dessert often served at a Burns Supper, Ceilidh Dinner or New Year's dinner. The raspberries can be layered with the cream mixture or combined together as in this recipe.

RECIPES

Cranachan (serves 4)

Ingredients
2-3 tablespoons of rolled oats
350g double cream
3 tablespoons of whisky
2-3 tablespoons of runny honey
300g fresh raspberries
(Keep some of the raspberries and rolled oats aside for topping.)

Method

Add the oats to a non-stick pan and stir over a high heat until the oats are toasted and crunchy. Leave to cool.

Place the double cream into a bowl and whisk until peaks start to form.

Gradually add the honey, whisky, raspberries and rolled oats to the mix (keeping some oats and raspberries aside for the topping). Mix gently until the ingredients are combined -without breaking up the raspberries too much.

Spoon into glasses.

Top with the extra raspberries and crunchy oats. Chill slightly before serving.

Creamy Whisky Sauce (Serves 2)

Whisky sauce is the perfect accompaniment to haggis. It can also be served with steak or chicken.

Ingredients

Knob of butter

3-4 tablespoons of whisky

50 ml of vegetable stock

1 teaspoon of Dijon mustard

100 ml of double cream

Method

Melt the butter in a frying pan. Add the whisky. Allow it to cook for a few minutes to burn off some of the alcohol. Then add the cream, stock and mustard. Whilst continually stirring the mixture, allow the sauce to thicken and reduce on a low heat. Place the warm whisky sauce into small jugs and serve with the haggis.

Chapter Two

THE GRAY STONE CROSS

Jeanne Swartz

Things are not all that they should be in the middle of tourist season at the Sunset Lodge, a tourist fishing destination on Alaska's Kenai Peninsula. What happened to Henry, the gentle but reclusive neighbour who lived down the beach and why is Oscar, Henry's sometime friend, sometime rival acting so strange? It is up to the lodge manager, Julia and her mother, Millie, to find out what happened to Henry and unravel the clues of the gifted salmon, the mysterious bloodstain, and the unusual cross formed out of stone.

I have no choice. I have to vanquish the dragon. I am triumphant when I force open the dragon's mouth and remove the threat. My reward is the sight of thirty bakery-style blueberry muffins, browned and fragrant, resting on the rack inside the oven, or, as I have named it, the dragon.

'I think the dragon changes its temperature to suit itself,' I said, 'and then the door locks up. I'm pretty sure that was what Alice was trying to tell you when she said it was haunted.'

'It's an oven. A mechanical apparatus. It doesn't have conscious thought.' Julia speaks in the reasonable tone she formerly used to soothe clients making million-dollar loan requests.

'When Alice insisted that the oven was haunted, it made no sense. Calling it a dragon is just as silly.'

'I know, Honey.' I set the muffins on the worktable. 'But it is so frustrating to see carefully prepared food come out overcooked or underdone for no reason. The oven seems to be directed by supernatural forces.'

'It's ridiculous,' Julia grumbled. 'Carol got that oven in a killer deal. Alice was just mad that she didn't get a say in the purchase but I can't believe she was upset enough to take off for a week. Right in the middle of tourist season.'

'There was probably a reason that Carol got a good deal on the oven. Whoever sold it to her likely knew it had problems. Alice will be back; she just needs to cool off. She knows Carol is doing everything she can to modernize the old lodge.' I surveyed the kitchen, noting how the sleek stainless-steel oven and dishwasher seemed out of place next to the chipped Formica counters and scarred wooden floors. The lodge owners, Rafe and Carol Moffit had made progress, but there was still much left to do.

The muffins had cooled, so I poured a tart lemon glaze over their domed tops. I said, 'Put these out on the sideboard. The guests will be down soon. The coffee is ready. I should have the eggs and bacon out in about twenty minutes.'

'Thanks, Mom,' Julia said as she gave me a quick hug. 'I don't know what I would have done if you hadn't been able to fill in when Alice left to find a spell that would work on a haunted oven.' She rolled her eyes and smiled.

'Glad to help,' I said.

'What did you pack for lunch?' Julia bent to look at the brown paper sacks lined up on the prep counter. Her green eyes glow under their long lashes.

I said, 'I made lunches they can eat while they hold their fishing poles. Crab salad sandwiches, apple slices, bags of chips, and ginger cookies. The cookies are there in case someone feels seasick.'

After breakfast, I handed out lunches and waved goodbye. It wasn't long until I heard the lodge skiff's motor growl. Julia used the skiff to ferry clients to meet the fishing charter boat anchored in deeper water. The guests could look back from the skiff to catch a good view of the lodge. The Sunset Lodge perched on a rocky shelf overlooking a long, curving beach. The two-story wooden structure had been built in an odd combination of Cape Cod and Northwest Regional architectural styles that somehow melded into a harmonious whole. Tall windows in the guest rooms and dining area faced west towards spectacular views of the volcanic peaks in the Chigmit Mountain subrange on the Alaska Peninsula, across the restless gray waters of Cook Inlet.

When I could no longer hear the skiff's motor above the rolling surf on the beach, I returned to my work in the kitchen. I was rooting through the walk-in cooler when I heard a distinctly canine whine followed by someone pounding on the kitchen door.

'No dogs in the kitchen.' I tried for an authoritative bellow but my words came out in an unladylike screech. I hurried to the kitchen door and pulled hard to ease it past the swollen wood on the door frame. My mouth fell open when I caught sight of the stranger standing outside. It was not the plumber I had been expecting. The visitor's head hung low on his neck. He wore dark green rain bibs and a mismatched rain jacket, the too-long sleeves rolled up at the wrists, showing cracks at the folds. Wisps of gray hair escaped under his odd, tri-cornered rain hat, blending in color and texture with strands from his unkempt beard. His dark eyes bored out from folds of wind-battered skin. Rainwater ran in streams and drips from every inch of his hunched figure. I must have stared at him for a full minute.

My scrutiny caused the man to scowl and shuffle his feet. 'Brought this for the girl,' he said, his voice like a file on rusty metal. I saw that he was holding a burlap sack. A very wet brown dog of an indeterminate breed crouched next to the sack, sad blue eyes regarding me with suspicion.

'Uh, what is it?' I said, undoubtedly confirming his opinion that I had no appreciable mental faculties.

'Salmon,' he said, handing me the sack. I noticed the man was missing two fingers on his right hand. My shoulder sagged under the weight of the sack's contents.

'For the girl,' he said again. 'She got my buggy going t'other day.'

I blinked. 'Do you mean Julia?'

'Yup.' Having completed his mission, he turned away, starting down the steps from the covered porch. The dog followed the man, tail drooping behind him.

'Thank you, Mister,' I called after him. 'Who shall I say dropped by?' I shouted these words at the figure moving across the lawn with a rapid stride. The stranger turned his head and replied. I wasn't sure I heard him because the falling rain muffled his voice. I stood at the open doorway, clutching the dripping burlap bag, watching him walk away.

'Tell me again, Mom. What did the man look like?'

Julia and I stood on the porch outside the kitchen, pitching our voices in low tones, even though no one was nearby. I described my visitor, repeating the name I thought I heard, 'Oscar.'

Julia looked down at the burlap sack I pulled from the walk-in cooler. She said, 'I cannot believe Oscar would part with a fresh-caught king salmon.'

'He said it was to thank you for helping him with his buggy.' I had already told her this but I wasn't sure she heard it.

'That's another weird thing.' She raised her chin to speak. 'Yesterday, I found Oscar out on the beach, next to his four-by-four,' using the local name for an all-terrain vehicle used for traveling on the local beaches. 'I stopped to see why he was standing there, and he told me he was stuck. It took me about a minute to figure out he had a bad spark plug and another two minutes to replace it. It was something Oscar could have fixed himself. It was almost like he was looking for a reason to stop me.' She frowned, remembering the encounter.

'Okay, but what do you want to do with this?' I pointed at the sack.

Julia grinned, that one-thousand-watt smile that had the power to melt my heart. 'Don't worry, Mom. I'll clean it and get the grill ready. We can have a salmon barbeque on the porch. Everyone will love it. I will fix it the way Henry showed me.'

I said, 'Henry, who?'

Julia pointed down the beach in the direction Oscar had taken when he left. 'Henry is a nice man who lives in a shack down the beach. I hope you get to meet him. He makes the best salmon barbeque ever.'

She was right. The grilled salmon with a miso maple glaze, a loaf of sourdough bread, and a big green salad were a big hit with the guests. After dinner, they toddled off to their rooms, yawning as they rubbed their stomachs with satisfaction.

Julia spoke up. 'Mom, how does a walk down the beach sound to you?'

Julia had little spare time, so I jumped at the chance to spend some time with her. My youngest daughter had her eyes fixed on a brilliant future since she had been in diapers. Julia worked hard to achieve her goals, earning a business degree and securing a position working in financial services. Climbing the company ladder was like riding a high-speed escalator for Julia and she seemed to relish her life, so I was shocked when she telephoned me one day from Fargo, North Dakota. Julia said she was returning to Alaska after accepting a severance package when her company merged with another firm. It was hard for me to believe my daughter was finished with the corporate world but when she met Rafe and Carol a few months later, it was clear she was serious. Carol had inherited her estranged father's fishing lodge and the couple decided to run it themselves as a modern, family-friendly venue. Julia agreed to work for them as a combination business manager, deckhand, and all-around handy-woman. I predicted disaster but as Julia fell more and more in love with the Kenai Peninsula's sweeping beaches and dramatic tidal swings, I accepted and eventually championed her chosen lifestyle. When she called me in a panic because the lodge chef, Alice, left for an impromptu vacation, I was happy to fill in for a few days.

Julia and I put on our rain gear and started walking down the beach. Low clouds obscured the view ahead, and our rubber boots squelched on gray, black, and white cobbles at our feet, shiny and rounded by surf action. The air was fragrant with the briny scent of seaweed and the sweet smell of rain.

'Are we going somewhere in particular?' I spoke after we left the lodge behind us.

'I want to talk to Henry about Oscar.' Julia had that obstinate tone in her voice I knew so well.

'Is this the same Henry who taught you how to barbeque salmon?'

'Yes. Henry lives next door to Oscar. They're not exactly friends; they do nothing but argue, but Henry would know what is going on with Oscar, like why Oscar gave me that salmon instead of selling it to a restaurant in Anchor Point. He could have gotten over a hundred dollars for it. Worth way more than a two-dollar spark plug.'

I shrugged, though the gesture was hidden under my rain coat. 'Maybe he was feeling generous.'

Julia's laugh was short. 'Oscar is the biggest miser ever born. He picks up bent nails and straightens them out. He never throws anything away. No way he would give away a valuable salmon.'

A shack made of mismatched plywood built on raised timbers appeared in a ghostly outline before us. Julia said, 'That's Oscar's place.' We took a few more steps, then a furious voice rang out, followed by the mournful howl of a dog.

'Stop right there. You're trespassing on private property.' We could just make out a hunched figure standing on the shack's uneven porch.

We stopped walking, and Julia cupped her hands over her mouth in a makeshift megaphone. 'Oscar. It's Julia from the lodge and my mom, Millie. You gave her the salmon this morning.'

After a brief silence, we heard another furious shout. 'Git back. Nothing here concerns you.'

Julia growled with exasperation. She shouted. 'We are on our way to see Henry.'

Instead of calming the old man down, her words caused him to reach into the open door and turn around with something in his hands.

'Julia,' I clutched her arm, 'I think he's got a gun.'

'Good grief,' Julia's face was pale under her rain hood. 'I wonder if he's having some kind of episode.' She raised her hands in a gesture of surrender. She shouted, 'We're leaving, Oscar. Put your shotgun away.'

Neither of us said much on the walk back to the lodge. I was shaken, but Julia seemed only worried and thoughtful. She halted a few times and turned to look back at Oscar's shack. We parted at the entrance to the lodge. As far as I was concerned, it had been too much excitement for one day.

&

The next morning, the rain had slowed to a drizzle. I saw no sign of Julia as I went into the kitchen to start making breakfast for the lodge guests. I began to worry about her when I heard familiar footsteps climbing the stairs to the back door of the kitchen. I called, 'Julia, where have you been?' I turned around so fast my ladle dripped pancake batter onto the floor.

My daughter came into the kitchen and washed her hands in the deep kitchen sink. Frown lines between her eyes dimmed her smile and her caramel-colored hair was windblown. She said, 'Here, Mom, let me get the sausages on the grill.'

I looked at Julia's reddened cheeks and said, 'You have been out on the water.'

'Something is going on with Oscar. That stunt he pulled last night has me worried. Oscar is a crotchety old cuss, but he has never been dangerous.'

I resumed pouring pancake batter on the spitting griddle. 'Please don't tell me you went to his place again this morning.'

Julia waved her hand at me and said, 'No, I took the skiff around to Henry's shack. I rowed into shore so Oscar wouldn't hear the motor.'

'Did you speak to Henry?' I watched the circles of batter on the grill fill the kitchen with a toasty, buttery scent.

'Henry was nowhere around.' She bit her lip, giving the sausages more attention than they needed. Julia turned to face me. 'Mom, Henry never leaves his shack, except maybe to go out fishing once in a while, and his boat is pulled up on the beach. He hates dealing with strangers. He doesn't have any family and except for Oscar and a few of us here on the beach, he doesn't interact with the outside world at all.'

I said, 'Maybe there was an emergency that made him leave.'

'I took a look around,' Julia said. 'Henry is compulsively neat. A chess board was sitting out and I saw a coffee cup on his kitchen table. Henry would never leave his things like that unless something was wrong.'

'Honey, you worry me. I hope you are not getting too involved.'

Julia continued as though she didn't hear me. 'I peeked out onto Henry's porch, the one that faces Oscar's cabin and I saw a red stain covering part of the boards. I'm afraid it might be blood.'

'Julia, you can't go back there. If you are so worried, you need to call the authorities.' I stepped away from the grill and wiped my hands on my apron, even though they were dry.

'Already called the Troopers, Mom.' Julia gave me a lopsided smile.

The guests were going into town to shop and eat lunch. After breakfast, the lodge's driver pulled up in the big van and everyone climbed in, exclaiming with excitement about the sunshine peeking out from the clouds.

We didn't have to wait long until a Dodge Charger with an Alaska State Troopers insignia pulled up to the lodge. I was mixing shortcakes for the guests' dinner dessert when I heard heavy footsteps on the stairs outside the dining room. I hurried out of the kitchen but Julia got to the door first. She stood in the doorway, speaking to a tall man wearing a blue uniform and a hat with a wide blue brim.

When I walked up to meet them, Julia said, 'Mom, this is Trooper Allen. He works out of the Anchor Point post. I told him about Henry.'

I turned to face a smile full of dazzling white teeth. Trooper Allen's shoulders were so broad they filled the doorway. His lively brown eyes moved around the dining room. He took off his hat with his left hand while he extended his right hand toward me. I was lost for a moment, gazing at his tanned face and the dimple on his chin.

Julia said, 'Trooper Allen is going down the beach to talk to Oscar.'

'You aren't going with him.' I looked at Trooper Allen and back at my daughter, my eyes wide.

'No, ma'am,' Trooper Allen assured me.

Julia looked disappointed but didn't protest. She left the dining area and headed toward the gear shed and I returned to the kitchen. It seemed like a long time before we heard footsteps approaching the lodge. Julia hurried to meet Trooper Allen. From my lookout at the kitchen window, I watched them talking. The discussion ended when Julia gave Trooper Allen a weak smile and he nodded and turned around. When I heard the Charger's engine come to life, I waited for her to come into the kitchen.

'What did Trooper Allen find out?' I knew my face was flushed.

She shrugged. 'He talked to Oscar but said Oscar knew nothing about Henry.'

'What about the bloodstain you thought you saw?' My voice was sharp.

'Oscar told Trooper Allen that Henry was cleaning fish on his deck and left the stain.' She added, 'Henry would never clean fish on his deck. I told him Henry was too tidy to do something like that, but it was my word against Oscar's.' Julia's face crumpled.

'Is that it?' Despite my resolve to stay out of it, I was uneasy.

'As far as he is concerned.' Julia jabbed her thumb in the direction Trooper Allen had taken.

'It took a while for him to tell you that he was done investigating.' I turned back to the sink and began to wash my hands.

'Oh, well, he asked me out.'

'What?' I left the water running in the sink and turned around, raising my eyebrows. 'Are you going to go out with him?'

Julia wore a grim little smile. 'I said that I couldn't think about a date until I knew what happened to Henry.'

The next morning, a heavy fog rolled in hard from the North Pacific. The tide was out so far we could hardly see where the water met the shoreline in front of the lodge. Our guests were scheduled to leave, so after a breakfast of Eggs Benedict and asparagus, Julia and I helped them load their fish and souvenirs into the van and said goodbye. We had a busy day ahead preparing for the next group of guests.

After the van left, Julia and I stood on the driveway. 'I'm going to town for groceries,' I said. She didn't reply, so I repeated myself. She was staring out at the water.

'Do you hear that?' Julia turned to me.

'Hear what?'

'It's Oscar's skiff. I would know that ratchety motor anywhere.' Julia turned and sprinted for the gear shed. I followed her at a trot, calling out questions as I went.

When I looked into the shed, I saw Julia pulling on her heavy rain gear and water boots. I stood with my hands on my hips and said in a tight voice, 'What are you doing?'

'Taking the boat out to follow Oscar.'

I cried, 'In this fog? Have you lost your senses?'

Julia paused, holding her rubber gloves in one hand. 'Mom, I know Oscar wouldn't go out in this weather unless he needed to hide something. And I am sure whatever he is hiding has to do with Henry.'

'Why do you have to do anything? Can't you call Trooper Allen?'

'I'm going.' Julia set her jaw.

I walked past her and started sorting through the rain gear hanging on the wall from wooden hooks. 'You're not going alone.' Julia got her stubbornness from me.

Together, we pulled the skiff across the exposed beach until we reached the waterline and Julia guided the boat into the inlet. She cut the motor frequently. From my seat in the bow, I could see the sides of her rain hat dip as she cocked her head, listening for the sound of Oscar's motor. The bow cut through the flat, olive-green water that seemed heavy, almost greasy, as we moved slowly through it. I was disoriented without landmarks, but I had faith that Julia knew where we were.

We moved ahead for what seemed like hours until Julia silenced the motor for the last time. She fitted oars into the oarlocks, rowing with a halting, yet silent motion. I heard the sigh of waves breaking somewhere ahead of us. One moment we were watching a gray curtain and the next minute the fog lifted and an eerie greenish light revealed a boat pulled up onto a flat shore.

Julia bent forward so I could hear her whisper, 'Oscar.'

We heard a grunting sound. A bent figure of a man came into view, moving along the shore in a hitching motion. The man was carrying something heavy, holding it in front of him with both hands. I recognized Oscar's tri-cornered rain hat. Julia and I watched him heave the load into his boat. We heard a dog yelp and saw a blur of brown fur leap toward the stern of Oscar's boat.

I couldn't help myself; I let out a cry of surprise. The sound carried across the water to Oscar, who straightened and stared at us.

Our cover was blown, so Julia called, 'Oscar, what are you doing?'

Oscar replied with a string of curses. Julia rowed the skiff forward, landing us on the low shoreline several yards from Oscar's boat. She jumped out and pulled the skiff forward. Now that we were upon it, I saw the shore was an island of muddy sand, barely higher than the waterline.

Julia turned to me. 'Stay here,' she said and then walked over to confront Oscar. She looked over the side of Oscar's boat and even through the lingering fog, I could see the puzzled look on her face. She turned to Oscar, and he began to speak, gesticulating furiously. Julia remained calm and said nothing.

My curiosity prodded me into motion. I climbed out of the skiff and walked over to Oscar's boat. When I looked over the side, I saw Oscar's brown dog sitting next to a large stone. It was a common type of dull-colored rock known as graywacke but was remarkable because of its unusual shape. Some long-ago glacial movement or tidal action had broken a large, flat rock into the perfectly formed shape of a cross measuring about three feet high and two feet wide. I was fascinated by the stone cross and didn't pay attention to Julia's and Oscar's conversation until she asked a question that made me look up with alarm.

'Where did you dump him?' Julia said, facing Oscar, their eyes locked together.

'What?' I stared at them. Oscar's and Julia's stances were mirror images, two figures in full rain gear, hands on hips.

'Ain't tellin." Oscar was unyielding.

'It's a crime.' Julia's voice cracked.

'So, call your Trooper boyfriend. He can arrest me.' Oscar gave Julia a look that was partly sneer, partly challenge.

'He's not my boyfriend,' Julia muttered.

'Julia,' I said, 'What is going on?'

'Look, Missy,' said Oscar, climbing into his boat, 'The tide's coming in. I'm leaving. Don't follow me.'

Julia gave a final despairing look at Oscar. To my surprise, she turned and trudged to our skiff. The exposed shoal had grown smaller in the time we had been there. Little waves were swallowing the sand. I turned and sloshed my way to where Julia was waiting for me.

Julia climbed in the skiff and frowned. 'Get in, Mom,' she said.

Seawater covered my ankles but I didn't move. 'I will get in when you tell me what is going on. What did you mean when you said Oscar was committing a crime? What is Oscar doing with that stone cross?'

'Get in the skiff, Mom,' Julia repeated. 'I will tell you what I know.'

The insides of my boots were getting wet, so I climbed over the bow and took my seat. We watched the silhouettes of Oscar and his dog disappear into the fog as our skiff lifted with the rising tide.

'Henry is dead, Mom,' Julia said softly.

I gaped at her. 'Dead?' I stuttered, 'D-did Oscar kill him?'

Julia sighed. She shook her head, and I could see her eyes were bright with tears. 'Oscar told me that Henry went out to fish a few days ago. When he returned, Oscar was working around his place. Henry came out on his porch to yell at Oscar for making too much noise. All of a sudden, he fell down. Oscar ran to help and found Henry almost unconscious on his porch, bleeding from a cut on his scalp.'

'The blood you saw on the porch.' I interrupted, my eyes wide. 'Did the fall kill him?'

Julia said, 'Oscar thinks Henry had a stroke or heart attack. He said the cut on Henry's head wasn't serious, even though it was bleeding heavily. He started to leave to get help, but Henry called him back. Henry was very weak and having trouble breathing but made Oscar promise to bury him at sea without, as Oscar said, getting folks all worked up.'

'What happened then?' As the fog drifted around us in phantom tendrils, I could not shake the feeling of other-worldliness.

Julia shrugged and said, 'Oscar stayed with Henry until he stopped breathing. He said he knew then that Henry was gone.'

'How could he be sure? Oscar isn't a doctor.' I was indignant. 'Didn't he even try to get help?'

Julia said, 'No. Oscar said he had made a promise to Henry and he knew he had to make good on it. He wrapped Henry up in an old sailcloth and dragged him to his boat to wait for high tide.'

'That's crazy.' My indignation turned to outrage. I balled my hands into fists and glared in the direction where we had last seen Oscar.

'I know.' Julia sighed again. 'But Oscar, well, he does things his own way. This all happened the same day I got his four-by-four going. I guess he had been keeping watch for intruders. Oscar fouled his own spark plug, knowing I would stop and help him. He didn't want me coming near his boat with Henry's body lying in it.'

'What happened to Henry?' I became aware that our skiff was drifting in erratic circles on the incoming tide.

Julia saw me looking at the water and tried to start the motor. It sputtered and died. She lifted up the cowling and began to fiddle with the mechanism. She said, 'Oscar said he had to wait until about four the next morning for high tide. He got an old crab pot out of that junk heap he keeps behind his shack and took it to his boat. Somehow, I don't know how, he was able to maneuver Henry's body inside it. He grabbed his trolling gear and launched his boat, with Henry's body in the crab pot balanced in the bow.'

'Gack,' I exclaimed. 'That is insane.'

Julia tried the engine again. It sputtered and died but it sounded less anemic. She returned her attention to the motor's inner workings. 'You have to understand that was the way Oscar thought. It seemed logical to him.'

I was almost afraid to ask my next question. I ventured, 'Did he, uh...?'

Julia's head was barely visible beneath the raised cowling. 'That's right. Henry is somewhere out there in a crab pot weighted with rocks.' She gestured toward the open inlet, holding a wrench in one hand. She tried the engine again. We were both gratified to hear it roar. Julia steered the skiff around and increased our speed until we were flying over the flat water.

I was rattled by Julia's story, mulling it over as we headed for the lodge. We had nearly arrived when I shouted a question, 'Did you say Oscar took fishing gear with him when he went out to bury Henry at sea?'

Julia gave a short bark that might have been a laugh. 'That's

Oscar for you. In case someone saw him out on the water after he, um, left Henry. Everyone around here knows Oscar wouldn't waste boat gas to just gallivant around. He put out a line to troll for salmon. He was more or less pretending to fish, but right away he hooked into a big salmon and---'

'He brought it to the lodge,' I finished.

'Yes. Oscar thought it was a sign that Henry was happy with what he had done, but he didn't feel comfortable keeping the salmon himself. He also thought it would be wrong to sell it. He definitely wasn't going to waste such a fine fish, so...' Julia didn't finish her sentence, just raised both hands in a gesture of acceptance.

I said, 'Now I feel funny about our merry feast the other night.'

'Me, too, a little,' said Julia. 'But Henry was a sweet old man. I think it would have pleased him to know he gave us so much enjoyment.'

When we reached the beach, Julia shut down the motor and raised the propeller. We jumped out of the boat and pulled it up the beach.

I had another question. 'What on earth was Oscar doing out there on the shoal today?'

'Oh, that.' Julia tugged on the mooring line, making sure it was fastened. 'When Henry first moved to the beach, he and Oscar became good friends. One day, they were out fishing and stopped at that shoal to fix something on Oscar's boat. Henry found that stone, the one you saw in his boat. Oscar was all for bringing it back and selling it. Henry wouldn't let him. Henry said that God put it there as a sign that this,' Julia made a broad gesture encompassing the beach and ocean, 'was a holy place and it wasn't right to disturb it. The two men argued about it for days and it became the sore point that started their feud. I guess Oscar went back to the shoal several times but could never find that stone cross. It really bugged him.'

I said, 'He found it today.'

'Yes,' Julia said. 'He said he had to wait for the combination of a very low tide and covering fog to try to find it again. When he got to the shoal today, he said he felt a presence lead him right to it.'

'Is he going to sell it now?'

Julia's chin quavered when she answered. 'No, he took it to give to Henry.'

We both stood in silence on the beach in front of the lodge. Overhead, the sun was breaking through the fog, shining silver and gold light in turn on the water. I said, 'Are you going to report Oscar?'

'I need to tell the troopers that Henry is missing. I'll leave it up to them to figure things out,' Julia said.

I arched a brow, 'I am getting the feeling now that you don't believe Oscar committed a crime.'

Julia looked down at her boots. 'I guess I've lived here at the beach too long. I'm starting to think like Oscar. I will leave it in God's hands. I think Henry would be okay with that decision.'

BIO:

Jeanne Swartz is an aspiring writer living and working in Anchorage, Alaska. Jeanne was among the contributors featured in the memoir anthology, *Anchorage Remembers: A Century of Tales*. Jeanne is currently working on her debut novel, a legal mystery set in Alaska, inspired by the people and places she has encountered in her travels. While living the dream in the 49th of the 50 United States, Jeanne has tried on many professional hats; at various times she has been employed as a forensic scientist, a classroom teacher, an oil company geophysicist, and an industrial facilities inspector and permit writer; but the constant in her life has always been her love of the outdoors in a cold climate.

RECIPE

Henry's Best Grilled Salmon

Ingredients

2-pound or 907 g salmon fillet or steaks, preferably wild-caught
Salt
Pepper
1 Tbs or 25 g white miso paste
1/3 cup or 80 mL maple syrup
2 Tbs or 20 mL citrus juice: lemon, lime, or grapefruit
Citrus slices, chopped parsley (optional)

Method

1. Pat salmon fillet or steaks dry. Remove pin bones from the fillet, if present. Sprinkle salt and pepper on the salmon. Set aside.

2. Warm maple syrup slightly. Remove from heat. Sir in miso paste until it almost completely dissolved, then stir in citrus juice.

3. Prepare a gas or charcoal grill with moderate heat (350-450 degrees F or 175 – 232 degrees C). Set a piece of aluminum foil on the grate. Or put the salmon under an oven broiler on a sheet pan with aluminum foil.

4. Lay the fillet or salmon steaks on the foil. If using a fillet, set it skin side down.

5. Pour or brush the maple-miso-citrus juice mixture on top of the salmon.

6. Cover and grill for 15 -20 minutes (fillet), depending on taste and the thickness of the salmon. If using an oven broiler, watch the salmon after about 8 minutes to make sure it doesn't overcook. The glaze may caramelize – that is okay.

Chapter Three

DEATH BY CAPPUCCINO

Sandra Ireland

In a quiet café, a simple cup of coffee sets off a chilling chain of revelations. As proprietor Laura turns detective in the hunt for a murderer, she must face the possibility that danger is a lot closer to home than she imagines and her past might hold the vital clue.

Laura Mulligan manoeuvred the heavy sign onto the pavement, choosing just the right spot to direct potential customers through the door of her coffee shop 'Brewed Awakenings.'

The sign read:

BEST COFFEE BREWED DAILY!

It featured an image of a foaming cappuccino and a crumbly scone. Who could resist? She straightened up and took a moment to gaze down the High Street. It was spitting rain, and the sky was dark, which might deter the average early morning shopper, but her regular customers were a hardy bunch. Laura had every confidence that they would appear in due course - Leo, after his stint at the gym; old Mrs Brennan, who turned her nose up at coffee and always insisted on tea; Marielle, Allan and of course dear Paul, who always made her smile. Laura had no family of her own. Her customers were her family.

She re-entered the shop, inhaling the pleasing aroma of roast beans and allowed herself to be pleasantly lulled by the hiss of the coffee machine. Her assistant was arranging the day's bakes in the glass display cabinet. Tazmin was biting her lip in concentration, all sharp elbows and stern expression, until, finally, she stepped back with a sigh that disturbed her bright blue fringe. Laura shook her head with a smile. Taz was her reluctant right-hand woman, her bad-tempered helper, but also the best barista in town. She was efficient, hardworking. Where would the café - and Laura be - without her?

She took a deep breath and approached the counter. Taz's moods were unpredictable, and now she folded her arms like a shield.

'These are yesterday's scones.' The girl made a face. 'Marielle should be here by now with the fresh ones.'

Like a scone, Taz was crusty on the outside, but she had a warm middle, if you took the time to find it. Laura had spent a lot of time trying to reach her, right from that first job interview, when Taz had spent the whole time twisting her nose stud and scowling at the tabletop.

'Nobody else would employ her,' Old Mrs Brennan had remarked darkly. 'You always end up with the waifs and strays.'

'She's not a waif or a stray,' Laura had responded. 'She's simply had a poor start in life and she's just come out of the care system. She needs a break.'

And Laura had given her that break. Taz had never thanked her, but she'd never let her down either, and she could pull a damn fine cup of coffee. She checked her watch.

'It's only a little after nine. You know what Marielle is like. Probably lost in meditation.'

Taz shook her head and went back to scouring the counter, as if the customers of Brewed Awakenings were, and always would be, a complete mystery to her.

They came in slowly, in dribs and drabs. First old Mrs Brennan, hanging onto the arm of Leo who ran the gym. They were a strange pairing, the stooped pensioner and the trendy young man with pronounced biceps and a trendy man-bun. But Leo was kind and caring. Laura admired how he'd dragged himself up from a difficult home life to become a businessman. He'd never forgotten his roots and did much to help the community, offering free boxing coaching to the youngsters who hung about the town centre. Paul Singh had helped him, of course. Paul had investments all over the region, and he had believed in Leo when many were just waiting for the boy to end up in jail like his father. Leo owed everything to Paul, his life, his sobriety and, if the grapevine was true, a good deal of money he was struggling to pay back.

Mrs Brennan shook the rain from her umbrella and spent five minutes complaining about the Scottish weather before Taz brought her a day-old scone in order to shut her up.

'That'll keep her mouth busy,' the girl growled in passing. Laura hid a smile and gently rebuked her.

'You'll be old yourself one day.'

'I won't grow old here, that's for sure. I'd be out of here like a shot, if I could afford it.'

Taz's constant threats to leave filled Laura with a chill she would not admit to.

Some five minutes later, Marielle turned up with the fresh scones and multiple apologies.

'I am so sorry, Laura!' Marielle's accent was French, and ridiculously attractive. 'I sat down to meditate for two minutes, and the time just went— *poof.*'

She made an elegant gesture with her fingers. Laura envied the woman's cute brunette plaits, her dusting of freckles and the way Paul touched her elbow as he made his way to his regular table.

'Do you want your usual, Paul?' Laura smiled sweetly at him.

'Oh, *Paul!*' Marielle twisted her fingers together. 'So 'andsome today in your suit! You 'ave a date, *non?*'

Paul's lusciously dark eyes softened with mirth.

'Not the sort of date you might think,' he said. 'Strictly business.'

He continued to his usual discreet booth to the rear of the shop. Leo used to sit with Paul most mornings, to discuss business, but Laura had noticed they'd been frosty with each other for a while now. Perhaps the rumours about unpaid debts were true.

Taz brought out Paul's cappuccino (extra chocolate) and one of Marielle's fresh batch of scones. Laura scowled as the French woman lingered by his table.

'I 'ad you in mind when I bake zem, Paul. Your favourite stilton and rosemary!'

The morning wore on. Laura busied herself making bacon rolls and hot chocolate for a family of four and several groups of friends turned up to exchange news over steaming flat whites. When she finally managed to draw breath, she realised that the place resembled a bomb site and duly dispatched Taz with a tray to clear up. The girl flounced away with such bad grace Laura was forced to hide a grin. Talk about having a chip on her shoulder! Taz's chip could be seen from space.

Presently the girl returned, her face paler than usual, so white, in fact, that her blue hair appeared almost fluorescent in contrast. Her eyes were bright with unaccustomed emotion.

'Laura,' she hissed. 'You'd better come. Paul is...*dead.*'

'Dead? How can he be dead?'

Laura's first sight of Paul sent her whole body rigid with shock, and it was a huge effort to reach out and touch the back of his hand where it rested on the table. He was still sitting upright, slightly slouched, sightless eyes trained on something he would never see. His skin was as pale as the foam on his cold coffee. Taz poked the sleeve of his suit.

'Is he cold?'

Laura searched for a pulse in his wrist, but her first aid qualifications were so sketchy she wasn't sure where to find it. Beneath her questing fingers there was only absence, his flesh as cool and waxy as a spent candle.

'Kind of, but he...he always complained of cold hands. He had bad circulation, a heart condition, but I think he was on medication.' Laura bit back a sob. 'He hasn't even finished his cappuccino!'

'Well, he won't be finishing it now,' Taz remarked bluntly, Laura bowed her head and gave in to tears.

'We have to call somebody.' She was dimly aware that her regular customers had gathered around her, full of questions and waiting for her to *do* something, but she felt paralysed. She'd always wondered how she'd behave in a crisis and now she was about to be tested. Now she was about to find out that she was useless, wallowing in her own shock.

'We need to call an ambulance.' Leo's voice seemed to come from a distance.

'Has anyone got a mirror?' Mrs Brennan piped up. 'To check for breath like they do in the movies?'

'He's definitely dead,' Taz said. 'He's as cold as his coffee.'

'Oh, Paul. *Paul!*' Marielle was sobbing openly, a tissue pressed to her face. 'He wouldn't 'arm a fly. Why zis?'

A new but familiar voice broke in, deep, comforting, in control. Retired Chief Inspector Allan Parks. He came in every day for his caffeine fix. Laura could have kissed him with relief.

'Let me see. I'll call some colleagues.'

He was the sort of crumpled, grizzled figure you could imagine ducking under a scene of crime tape. His whole being shouted *I'm in charge, nothing to see here*. He did the required medical checks with the sort of cool efficiency that Laura could only dream of. She garbled a series of explanations that sounded increasingly like excuses. *He was right as rain...drinking his coffee... nobody saw that coming...*

Why did she suddenly feel guilty? Because it had happened on her premises, and on her watch. It was unprecedented. Customers simply did not drop dead over their coffee cups. Was something else going on here? Something sinister?

Her mind spun back forty minutes. A man had breezed in. She'd been busy so she couldn't recall his features; she was as poor a witness as she was a first aider. But the more she thought about it, the more certain details sprang to mind- a battered leather jacket and a shock of unruly salt and pepper hair, an impression of strength and purpose. Definitely purpose. He'd strode straight up to Paul's table, but he hadn't stayed long enough to even sit down, never mind order a drink. Just the sort of customer she could do without, she'd thought waspishly at the time, but what if...what if this was some gangland boss or some loan shark demanding money? Paul was known to have a finger in every pie. What if some of his business dealings had gone sour?

Allan began ushering the other customers towards the door.

'Let's give the paramedics a bit of space. Yes, yes, you can come back tomorrow.' He brooked no argument, and even Mrs Brennan shrugged into her coat with a minimum of fuss. Leo went out onto the street to flag down the ambulance.

Allan strode back to Paul's table, brow furrowed.

'There was a man...' Laura stammered. 'Earlier on. A man in a leather jacket.'

'Did they have a conversation?'

'I'm not sure. I was busy.'

'It could be nothing, but tell my colleagues when they arrive. One thing though...where are his empties?'

Laura's gaze snapped back to the table. A brown ring and a trail of crumbs were all that remained of Paul's elevenses.

'Oh...Taz must have cleared up. He'd only had half a cup of coffee and a scone.'

Allan nodded. 'What a waste.'

Laura couldn't tell if he was talking about the food or the man.

The next forty minutes passed in a blur. Laura had to endure the agony of watching poor Paul wheeled out to the waiting ambulance. She didn't want to look, but neither could she drag her eyes away, and afterwards, all she could remember were Paul's flaccid hands lying beside him; hands which had stroked her face and lovingly caressed her. She longed for one more glance from those passion-filled eyes, but his blue-tinged lids stayed firmly shut, long lashes two black arcs against his ashen cheeks. After he was gone, Laura remained glued to the spot, chewing the skin around her fingernails until it was red-raw. Her mouth was dry, but she needed something stronger than water. She just wanted to go home and pour herself a large Scotch, and she never drank spirits.

'I'd better get going then,' Allan said. 'Will you be okay?'

Laura came back to life with an effort. All around her were forlorn reminders of what had just transpired; a discarded latex glove, one of Paul's shoes that had slipped off during transit and a melee of urgent wet footprints patterning the floor. Automatically, Laura went to get a mop. Now that the initial rush of horror had passed, she felt deflated, unsure of what to do next. Allan was staring at his phone, lost in thought. Laura's mind skittered like a pebble over a sea of criminal possibilities. The man in the leather coat, Marielle's tears and the comment she'd made about Paul not deserving such a fate. That sounded like an accusation, as if something sinister had struck him down, and not simply the failed workings of his own heart.

Laura put down the mop and went behind the counter. Paul's coffee cup and half-eaten scone sat where Taz had abandoned them. That was surprising, as the girl was ultra-efficient, but the attending police officers had chased everyone out. Her apron had been flung carelessly to the floor. Laura picked it up. On a sudden whim, she popped the half-eaten scone into a plastic jiffy bag and the coffee dregs into a spice container which she'd sterilised with boiling water. Rounding the counter, she proffered them to the retired detective. He gazed at the items for a second before taking them.

'You still have contacts in the lab, don't you?' She murmured.

'I do.' He stowed the specimens in the capacious pocket of his overcoat. 'You've been reading too much Agatha Christie.'

Laura shook her head. 'I just know that Paul's heart condition was under control. He was on medication. This doesn't make sense.'

'Maybe his number was up. Who are we to say? But...' He patted his pocket, his granite face softening for a second. '...I will get these tested. Just to set your mind at rest.'

After Allan left, Laura realised there was one more thing she needed to do for Paul. She searched her handbag for the key to his apartment, put on her coat and let herself out of the café, locking the door behind her. Paul had a cat, Henry, who would need feeding and consoling. Laura always looked after Paul's home when he was away, hence the key. It was the least she could do for him now. She would make sure that Henry was fine and that Paul's home was tidy for whatever was to come next. He'd never spoken about close family, but presumably someone in authority would have to hunt down his next-of-kin to make the necessary arrangements. Misery as dark as the stormy sky welled up inside her as she marched towards the smart crescent where Paul lived. She couldn't believe she would never see him again. She'd miss his face, his gentle smile, the warm buzz she experienced when he entered the café. Tears rolled unchecked down her cheeks.

Paul's building was a grand Edwardian conversion, and his flat was on the second floor. Laura knew the entry code off by heart. The smart marble lobby echoed with her footsteps as she made her way up the stairs. Feeling for the key, she prepared to open the apartment door, to call for Henry, and tell him everything was going to be okay.

Laura's heart skipped a beat. The door was already ajar.

Holding her breath, she gave it a push, and the gap widened to reveal an expanse of tasteful, monochrome hallway, with Paul's snow white cat sitting at the far end, calmly licking one paw. Henry didn't seem unduly stressed. Had Paul simply left without locking up? It seemed unlikely. He was - *had been* - fastidious in all matters of security. Against her better judgement, Laura took a step inside, leaving the exit open, just in case. Henry lowered his paw with a curious mew. She was about to call out to him when a noise alerted her to a doorway on the left. Paul's study. An intruder was in Paul's study!

Every instinct screamed at her to flee, but she stayed rooted to the spot. Only her lungs remained active, panting for breath as her heart tripled its rhythm. The rustle of papers came from the room, and a faint cough, as if the unseen trespasser had dislodged some dust. Should she call out, make her presence known? She couldn't just run away and leave a burglar rooting through Paul's things!

Suddenly, a figure emerged from the study. Laura gasped. It

was the man in the brown leather coat. He seemed equally surprised to see her standing there, running his fingers through his hair until it bristled alarmingly. He spoke first; Laura was still open-mouthed with shock.

'Aren't you the woman from the café?'

'I might be.'

'What are you doing here?'

'What are *you* doing here?'

'I have a key.'

'*I* have a key.'

The impasse shimmered between them. Eventually, the man threw up his hands in defeat.

'Look, let me introduce myself. I'm Larry Hagg. Paul's solicitor. I was looking for his Will. We'd arranged a meeting to discuss some particular amendments but...it wasn't meant to be. I cannot believe he's gone.'

'Wait. How did you know...?' Laura glanced quickly behind her as if the drama of the last few hours was writ large upon the walls.

'Bad news travels fast,' Larry said. He was tall, and unkempt in a very styled sort of way, with an artfully knotted scarf about his throat. The leather jacket was vintage, rather than merely scuffed. 'Anyway, I found the Will among my client's papers. I need to notify the executor. It's my duty to see to Paul's affairs. It's an utter tragedy.'

The last sentence seemed a bit forced to Laura's ears, as if he were the sort of man who put business first and emotion second. Wasn't it a strange coincidence that Larry Hagg had been the last person to see Paul alive? Had they spoken about something so shocking that it had resulted in a massive heart attack? Laura started to run through the possibilities - financial ruin, a lawsuit - but Larry Hagg was preparing to leave, and she doubted he'd share the content of their final conversation with her.

'I came to feed the cat,' she said lamely.

Larry glanced at Henry, who was still sitting in the same spot.

'Oh good. I did wonder. Are you happy to continue with that then? Until we sort out the estate?'

'Yes, yes...I'll see to it.' The sadness came over her again, a dull wave. Nothing would ever be the same again. Without Paul, the axis of her life had suddenly shifted. True, they hadn't been an 'item' for many years, but he had still been a presence in her life.

The solicitor left, apparently satisfied that Laura was not an intruder bent on nefarious deeds. She went into the kitchen and automatically found the cat food and the bowl and the spoon. Being acquainted with the spoon a person used for their cat food was an odd kind of intimacy. Henry rubbed around her legs and purred so loudly the sound echoed in the tidy kitchen. Everything was put away, towels neatly folded and the sink empty, as if Paul had some inner knowing that he would never return to this place.

Leaving Henry to his food, Laura wandered through to Paul's study. It seemed an affront to go in there, so instead she lingered at the door for the longest time. Like the kitchen, the room was immaculate, save for some loose paperwork scattered on the mahogany desk. Larry Hagg could at least have tidied up after himself. She didn't know the protocols of such an event, but it didn't seem appropriate for your solicitor to be poking around in your affairs in the immediate aftermath of your demise. She shuddered and approached the desk.

There were a couple of red cardboard folders, the kind you buy in packs of five. They were dog-eared and worn, with scribbled-out labels as if they'd been repurposed more than once. The first, and she felt ashamed to be prying, held a series of utility bills. The second, a small pile of personal correspondence, stamped and addressed. It was quaint. Who writes letters anymore?

She picked up the first envelope. It was a thin, cheap, white one, with a local postmark. The writing was angular, but neat. Blue biro. It seemed familiar, but she couldn't place it. Handwriting was barely a thing anymore. She recalled the comfort of seeing her late mother's handwriting in old recipe books. She'd always thought it a pleasure that would be denied to the younger generation. They would never know that connection, because they never wrote things down.

She pulled the letter from the envelope and began to read.

Paul,

Since you ignored my last letter, I thought I'd try again. I understand it must have been a shock to receive it, but what about me? How do you think I feel? It took me so much courage to write it - please do not reject me again.

I have already given you my number. I'm waiting for your call.

There was no signature, just a round frowny face and a single kiss. Laura thrust the letter back into the envelope. It felt horribly private and painfully obvious. She knew that handwriting. There *was* one person who still penned things by hand, a person who delivered a scribbled invoice on the last day of every month.

Laura's suspicions about Paul's scone had been validated. Stilton and rosemary indeed. Stilton and death, more like. There was no time to lose. Laura shoved the letters into her shoulder bag and left the apartment at top speed.

'Are you going to let me in?' Laura struck what she hoped was a vaguely threatening pose.

Marielle hovered in her cottage porch, biting her lip. A cloud of fragrant incense wreathed her in a mystery that Laura was determined to crack.

'Actually, I was meditating, Laura. It is not a good time. I was lighting a candle for poor Paul.'

Laura stepped past her, made her way through the boxes of homegrown vegetables that cluttered the small space. Onions hung from the beams, and herbs flourished in terracotta pots.

'It's about Paul. That's why I'm here. I found a letter among his things.'

Marielle sighed and shrugged, tucking a strand of dark hair behind one ear.

'You had better come in.'

Inside, a wall of serenity met Laura. The soft cushions in the sitting room, the fragrance, the sounds of whale music... She could not imagine living in such a tranquil bubble. Was Marielle so divorced from reality she could contemplate killing a man who'd spurned her in cold blood?

'I think the letters were from you.'

'Letters?'

'There was more than one.'

'And you have read them all?'

'No,' Laura admitted. 'But I got the gist of them. It's a story as old as time. Woman chases man, man rejects woman, woman makes threats...'

'So, the letters are threats?' Marielle pulled a puzzled face. Even when she was scowling she still looked cute, dammit. Laura had to admit to a certain satisfaction that Paul had rejected such delectable being, but it should not have cost him his life.

'Not a threat, exactly,' Laura said carefully. 'Perhaps more of a plea from the heart, a *cri du coeur.*'

'Ah! That language I understand.' Marielle chuckled at her own joke, before correcting herself. '*Mais* this is not funny. The heart will stop at nothing to get what it wants.'

They were still standing, Laura noted. She hadn't been offered a seat. The atmosphere between them was tense to say the least, but that was to be expected. She had just basically accused the woman of murder. Marielle moved to the sideboard, opened a drawer and extracted a notebook.

'You have the letter, *oui*? Then please to compare the hand-writings.'

Laura realised she should have done that first. It would have made more sense than turning up unannounced with such a savage accusation. Reluctantly, Laura pulled one of the letters from her bag and extracted the note from its envelope. She weighed it against the pages of the open notebook that Marielle was proffering. They both studied in silence for a second.

'*Non,* see the 'c's, that squiggle on the end? They are completely different and the 'a' - here and here. I write my 'a' like *so*, and not like *this*.'

Red shame bloomed at Laura's neckline. It was true. Marielle's handwriting ruled her out of the mad, bad equation in Laura's head.

'I'll have to do some more homework,' she said tightly.

'You think Paul was murdered? You think I killed him?' Marielle's lower lip quivered. Anxious not to remain on the scene for another fit of weeping, Laura made her excuses and left, apologising as she went. So sorry for calling unannounced. No, she'd never seriously suspected Marielle. She was just trying to make things add up, and no, she did not think that Paul died of natural causes.

Marielle's words followed her through the cottage gate.

'What about Leo? Leo owed Paul a lot of money.'

It wasn't as if Laura hadn't thought of that, but Leo was strong, tough and from a family that could hold their own on the street corner and the boxing ring. If Leo wanted someone out of his hair, he would surely have dreamed up a more violent, desperate end? Leo's name was still scrawled on the whiteboard in her brain, but it was far down the list, behind Larry Hagg and Marielle, although Marielle had now dropped down a place. Who was topping the list of suspects?

A certain possibility was beginning to take root in the cracks like a scarlet poppy, a big red flag. It couldn't be, could it?

Laura mulled over this possibility throughout her fifteen - minute walk back into town. It hurt her skull to think of such a thing. Reluctantly, she let herself back into the dark, deserted café. There was something eerie about being there alone. It felt as if the day's horror had permanently tainted the atmosphere. Laura could almost feel the presence of Paul lurking in the gloom, as if reluctant to move on until she'd made a breakthrough.

'I will find out. Paul,' she whispered. 'I will get justice for you.'

Her phone pinged with a message from Allan. Like the detective, it was blunt and to-the-point.

Initial medical findings suggest heart issues.

Laura made a face and put the phone back in her bag. That could mean anything. She'd reserve judgement until the toxicology results came back. Allan would surely be able to pull a few strings in order to make that happen. But first, she had to set her mind at rest. The puzzle of the handwriting was pulling and probing at her, refusing to release its grip. There was another name out there, daring her to grasp it. Laura approached the spike on the counter where all the service dockets from that day awaited disposal. Taz had a habit of jamming her table orders on there with such force it was a miracle she'd never stabbed her hand.

With a feeling of cold dread, Laura lifted one of the dockets and scanned the legend.

Cappuccino x 1

Scone x 1

She extracted one of Paul's letters from her bag and spread it out on the counter. There was the 'a' and the squiggly 'c', just as Marielle had noted, but the writing on this note was a perfect match.

Laura dropped both pieces of paper onto the counter and backed away. *Deep breath*. It was okay. This did not mean anything. This did not mean that Taz, her beloved Taz, was involved with any crime. It *did* mean, however, that she was linked to Paul in the most unbelievable way.

The implications of that particular relationship made Laura weak and breathless. She collapsed into the nearest chair and slowly pulled the remaining letters from her bag. Checking the date stamps, she assembled them in order.

If there was a story here, she would need to start at the beginning.

Dear Paul,

You do know me, but not in the way you're about to discover.

You know me as Taz, the girl who makes your coffee and brings you scones. I guess you barely spare me a thought. However, what you need to know about me is this.

When I was born, I was put up for adoption. The usual story, I guess. Woman gets pregnant, can't cope, and the father is nowhere to be seen. Only, you were somewhere. Yes, Paul. When I turned 18, I set about finding my birth parents and the DNA computer base flagged up a direct link to you.

You are my father, Paul! Hiding in plain sight behind your daily cappuccino. I know it is a lot to take in, but I hope we can be friends, at least. Get to know each other. I thought writing a letter might be a gentler way of breaking the news. I will include my mobile number. Please call me.

Love Tazmin.

Laura lowered the note to the table, where it fluttered in her trembling hands. Not Taz! Surely Taz could not have been involved in Paul's untimely death? The motive was there, the child twice rejected by a parent- but surely the girl wasn't capable of such evil? However, the thirst for vengeance could drive out rational thought.

No one must know of this! It would be business as usual until more evidence presented itself. Laura scrambled together the letters, thrust them into her bag and buckled the flap, as if by some trickery they might crawl out and alert the world to Taz's unfortunate circumstances. The girl had been shocked upon finding Paul's lifeless body but, Laura noted, she'd never shed a tear over him. She had not been visibly upset and it was Taz who had whisked away the remains of Paul's snack. Did that point to her guilt like a bloodied hand?

Laura had only three days to wait for some kind of closure. On the third day, a little before opening time, Allan Parks tapped discreetly on the glass door of the cafe. Laura hurried to let him in. She knew why he was there; his grim face said it all.

'Laura, don't breathe a word of this to anyone. The case is in the hands of the Murder Investigation Team and you'll be getting an official visit shortly, but...'

Laura held her breath. She had always known what he was going to say. His next words did not surprise her. They landed before her like heavy stones.

'The initial toxicology report has found traces of oleander in the dregs of Paul's cappuccino. The hows and whys of how that ended up there are questions for another day, but I just wanted you to know, so you can think about protecting yourself. Paul was poisoned. Oleander is a powerful plant that can exacerbate an existing health condition. All parts of it are lethal and in Paul's case, it brought about instantaneous death. The big question is- and one which the cops will be asking is - who the hell would want to do such a thing?'

Laura's breath left her body. She thought of the incriminating letters nestling in her handbag like vipers.

'I have no idea,' she said faintly. 'Paul was a lovely guy. Perhaps it was an accident. Maybe the culprit didn't know what she...he...they were doing?'

'Oh, this was deliberate,' Allan scoffed. 'Anyway, I can't stop. But be on your guard, Laura. Someone you know likely did this.'

Some of the regulars began to drift in after that. Leo and Mrs Brennan chose a table as far away as possible from Paul's booth. They were subdued, chatting quietly, their gazes straying occasionally in Laura's direction as she worked behind the counter. Were they talking about her? Did they think she had a hand in this? In a way, perhaps she did. If she had lived her life differently, made better choices, but oh...what's done is done. You cannot relive your life.

By ten a.m. it was obvious that Taz was not going to show up for work, and her phone was going straight to voicemail. The girl had made good her threat. She'd left, without a backward glance or a word of goodbye. Perhaps she wanted to evade the law, or maybe she was sick and tired of never fitting in. Her whole life had been a series of council facilities and foster families with no ties to her. Is it any wonder that she finally flipped? She had probably been dreaming of meeting her parents her whole life, and when she finally did track down her father, Paul, he didn't want to know. It was enough to drive anyone to murder.

Last night, Laura had read the final note in the series Taz had sent Paul.

You have had your chance. After knowing this, I served you coffee today, and you didn't even make eye contact. Be warned, Dad. I will make you pay for what you have done. And when I find my mother, she will pay too.

Laura had pressed the page to her heart, feeling its scared, uneven hammering. It felt like a death knell, as if she had come to the end of something, all those years of subterfuge and denial. She could no longer live a lie, but she didn't know how to put things right. Everything had gone horribly wrong. She'd thought, by giving Taz the job, she'd be keeping her close, right in the bosom of their little café family. It had felt like the right thing to do, the only thing. She never thought the truth would come out in such a brutal way.

Now, she spared a thought for Paul's heart and how it had reacted to the poison administered by his own daughter. *Their* daughter. One day soon, Taz would discover the truth about who her mother was.

One day soon, she would come back for Laura.

BIO:

Sandra Ireland is the author of five psychological thrillers and works as a creative writing facilitator. Residing on Scotland's east coast in a historic fisherman's cottage, she loves to write short stories and poetry inspired by the Scottish landscape. Her latest novel, *The House on Devil's Lane,* is out now.

https://sandrairelandauthor.com/

RECIPE

Banana and Coffee Loaf

A simple banana and coffee loaf. Perfect for using up any over-ripe bananas.

Ingredients
3 ripe bananas, peeled and chopped
110g soft brown sugar

1 tablespoon of instant coffee dissolved in a small amount of
boiling water
85g of melted unsalted butter (additional butter to grease the
loaf tin)
225g self-raising flour
2 beaten eggs
Pinch of cinnamon
Pinch of salt

Method
Preheat the oven to 190 or 170 fan-assisted /gas mark 5
Grease a 1-litre loaf tin
Mash the bananas in a bowl
Add the sugar, eggs, coffee, cinnamon and salt, and mix until all
the ingredients are combined.
Fold in the butter and sieved flour.
Stir the mixture
Pour the mixture into the greased loaf tin and bake for 50
minutes (until a skewer comes out clean when inserted into the
middle of the loaf).
Leave to cool on a wire rack and serve in slices.

Chapter Four

THE FINAL FLAMBÉ

Lisa Knudsen Harkrader

Teddy Blake, washed-up child actor, thought sending his old producer anonymous tickets to his performance on a murder mystery dinner train might reignite his career. But when a guest dies - for real - and the audience thinks it's part of the script, Teddy must scramble to hide the body, solve the murder, and stay in character before dessert is served and the train pulls into the station.

Supper Sleuths Rocky Mountain Express
presents
LAST WILL AND TREACHERY
directed by Simone Langston

Olivia, ~~gold-digging~~ grieving widow LYDIA LIN

Reggie, estranged sonMALIK HAYES

Amelia, loyal but penniless nieceKIT RILEY

Leland Carrington, family lawyer DESMOND CROSS

Baxter, the butlerTEDDY BLAKE

Cook, the cookMAVIS DILLARD

The Victim*TO BE DETERMINED - BY MURDER!*

Setting: Winterhaven Manor in the snowy Rockies, where patriarch Alistair Van Winter has recently drawn his last breath. His family and household staff have gathered for the reading of his will, only for secrets to spill, tempers to flare - and murder to strike.

Can you solve the mystery before the train reaches its final destination?

I smoothed the lapels of my tailcoat. It was worn at the cuffs and gave off a whiff of *eau de musty wardrobe department*. I cut a look at my reflection in the stainless-steel door of the walk-in fridge. In the flickering LED candlelight of the dining car, I'd still pass as a dignified, slightly cheeky butler.

'Relax, Boy Detective.' Malik clapped a hand on my shoulder. 'You still got it.'

I shot him my signature Teddy Blake half-grin. I *did* still have it.

I let the grin fade.

I just hoped somebody still wanted it.

I lifted the edge of the heavy velvet curtain so we could sneak a peek at the dining section. The six-top VIP table - best seat in the house - was still two-thirds empty.

Where *was* she?

Malik tipped his head toward the two guests seated there. 'Which one's getting offed tonight?'

I frowned. I hadn't really been paying attention. Neither of them were Veronica Chase.

But now I studied them. A girl, late twenties, perched on the edge of her chair taking in every detail, her dark curls quivering with excitement. Beside her sat an older dumpling of a woman - flowered dress, crocheted cardigan - scribbling in a notebook. They'd boarded first and now sat in the seats reserved for the winner of the Supper Sleuths Ultimate Detective Experience and her plus-one.

'My money's on the younger one,' I said.

'She seems pretty pumped,' said Malik. 'Oh, my god.' He looked closer. 'Is she wearing a *ClueQuest* t-shirt?'

I peered out. Oh god. She was. I closed my eyes.

Full disclosure: I'm famous. Well, used to be. I starred as kid detective Teddy Keene in the popular cable show *ClueQuest*. For four years I solved tricky mysteries like the Great Bake Sale Sabotage and Phantom of the Science Fair.

It was a sweet gig: magazine covers, on-set tutors, catchy theme song.

Then puberty hit like a brick, and I got written out of my own show.

Two shrill blasts of the train's horn echoed through the dining car. The train lurched, my heart lurching with it. I braced a hand against the fridge as it began its gentle rocking, the rhythmic *chuff-chuff-chuff-chuff* picking up speed.

Malik followed my gaze toward the still nearly empty table.

'It was always gonna be a long shot.' He bumped my shoulder. 'Madam Cutthroat's tough to impress.'

I nodded. But didn't look at him. I'd had enough pity the last fifteen years.

Malik and I and the rest of the cast were crowded into the food staging area between the dining room and the galley. On cue, Chef Anton emerged from the galley - his tiny kingdom of sharp knives, sizzling pans, and increasingly impressive curse words - to set out trays of champagne. We found our trays and took a moment to draw cleansing breaths and buzz our lips in warmup.

Because in a dinner train show, you're always in character. Pulling out a guest's chair? You're still playing Leland Carrington, Van Winter family lawyer. Clearing plates? You're Olivia Van Winter, not-so-grieving widow. Serving champagne from a fake-silver tray? You're doing it as Baxter the butler - me.

I hoisted my tray and stepped out from the curtain.

My station was the six-top VIP. I'd made sure of that when I'd first hatched my no-fail comeback plan. As I made my way down the narrow aisle, swaying with the train, two things happened.

The girl in the *ClueQuest* shirt squealed, 'Teddy Blake! Oh, my god!'

Behind me, another voice growled, 'Teddy Blake? Oh, dear *god*.'

I froze. I was the one who'd - anonymously, of course - sent her the tickets for tonight's show. I thought I'd be prepared.

But I turned, and there she was. Veronica Chase. And suddenly I was thirteen again, holding a script I'd never get to shoot, ugly crying in my mom's Hyundai.

She swept down the aisle, designer silk flowing over sharp angles - sharp cheekbones, sharper eyebrows, sharply angled hair - casting her sharp gaze like a machete, slashing everything in its path.

Luckily, we were on a moving train. The champagne glasses clinking on my trembling tray seemed normal.

She flicked me a once-over. 'You're looking. . . well.' She pushed past to her seat.

A young woman scurried behind, fluffing Veronica's scarf, stowing Veronica's purse, unfolding Veronica's napkin. Had to be Veronica's latest PA. She couldn't have been on the job long. A blotchy red rash was creeping up her neck, but she looked like she still had a sliver of hope.

As she took her own seat, I frowned. Something about her seemed familiar.

'*Teddddy*.'

A hand smacked me on the back. I glanced around.

And nearly choked.

Zacky.

Templeton.

Remember when I said I was axed from my own show? Veronica did the axing, and Zacky's who she replaced me with. Zacky and I filmed exactly one episode together, the one where Teddy Keene's younger cousin (Zacky) moves in with Teddy's parents, steals Teddy's friends, and starts solving Teddy's mysteries. Meanwhile, Teddy's packed off to boarding school, never to be seen again.

Zacky looked me up and down, taking in the bowtie, white gloves, waiter's cloth draped over my arm. 'Good to see you're still, ah, working.'

He flashed a smirk in Veronica's direction, then slid into the seat on the other side of her.

Behind him strode a guy in a slim-cut suit and black t-shirt. He flipped off his completely unnecessary Ray-Bans, and I recognized him too: Craig Loomis, my old agent. He'd dumped me right after Veronica did.

I took a breath. Veronica. Zacky. Craig. Plus, the overeager fan in the *ClueQuest* shirt. It was the reunion from - I don't even know where. What's worse than hell? An open casting call? It was the reunion from there.

Malik was serving at the next table. '*Free anonymous tickets*,' he murmured. '*My big chance to impress her. Once she sees my performance, she'll have to cast me in her new show. What could go wrong?*'

Nothing. I squared my shoulders. I had two hours before the train pulled into the station. Two hours to do what I'd set out to do. Two hours to convince Veronica I was the actor she needed.

I fixed my guests with a condescending gaze.

'Welcome to the Winterhaven,' I said, in the stuffy deadpan of a long-suffering manservant. 'Where the wine is vintage, the secrets refuse to stay buried, and the help is tragically underpaid. I'm Baxter, at your service.'

I began placing champagne before each guest, beginning with Veronica, then moving to her PA.

'Miss.' I set a glass before her.

'Emily.' She fidgeted. 'I'm—'

'For Pete's sake, Emily.' Veronica huffed in disgust. 'He doesn't need to know that. He's here to serve our food and apparently' - she flicked a look at me - 'entertain us.'

Emily swallowed, her blotches creeping into the roots of her coppery hair.

I moved around the table, placing a glass before the *ClueQuest* fan.

'I can't believe I'm actually here.' She pressed her hands to her chest and gazed at me, eyes wide. 'In the presence of Teddy Blake.'

I wanted to tell her to relax, that meeting me wasn't a big deal.

Zacky must've agreed. I heard him groan.

'I used to write you letters after every show.' She blinked up at me. 'Maybe you remember - Paisley Perez? Aunt Mags said you probably wouldn't. You get so much fan mail. Oh!' She patted the dumpling woman next to her. 'This is her. Aunt Mags. She's never seen your show – *sorry* - but she's big into mysteries.'

Aunt Mags jotted something in her notebook, then looked up and smiled.

'Ms. Perez.' I tipped my head. 'Your enthusiasm is appreciated. Miss Mags, no previous series knowledge is necessary, though early seasons held a certain charm that was sadly lacking after the ill-advised casting shake-up.'

Aunt Mags let out a titter. Paisley fairly swooned. Zacky narrowed his eyes in confusion, like he knew I'd insulted him but hadn't worked out how. From the corner of my eye, I saw Veronica almost smile. Inwardly, I smiled too. I'd timed it well. There was nothing Veronica Chase loved more than petty snark.

As I approached Craig Loomis, he slid a vape pen from his jacket.

He raised his eyebrows. 'I don't suppose. . . ?'

'I'm afraid not, sir,' I said. 'Nicotine products are strictly prohibited.'

'I figured.' He sighed and slid the vape into his jacket.

I placed the final champagne flutes. 'Mr. Loomis. Master Zacky.'

'Zacky?' Paisley Perez wrinkled her brow. 'But you - you're – ' She pulled out her phone and began furiously thumb-typing. She stared up at Zacky. 'You're the backstabber who wormed his way into Teddy's life, then pushed him off the show. Zacky Templeton.'

She thrust her phone, open to Zacky's IMDb page, into his face.

Zacky pulled back. 'Hey.' He held up his hands. 'I'm just the actor. Teddy's exit was an executive-level decision. Totally out of my hands. Also, I go by Zac now.'

'Executive?' Paisley began tapping her phone again.

She looked up, this time at Veronica.

'*You* did it,' she said, her voice a betrayed whisper. '*You're* the backstabber.'

'Oh, aren't you adorable?' Veronica wrapped manicured fingers around the stem of her glass. 'Look, television's a business. A dog-eat-dog business sometimes, sure, but Teddy aged out, and Zacky tested well with the under-twelve demo. It was that simple. Cheers.'

As she raised her glass, a voice rang out.

'Ladies and gentlemen—'

Everyone turned as Simone Langston breezed through the dining car.

'—welcome aboard. I'm Simone Langston, director of this evening's performance.' She turned a circle, smiling at the guests. 'Tonight, you'll enjoy delicious food, a deadly mystery, and, if you're sharp, an opportunity to solve it before dessert. Bon appétit, and remember—'

Her gaze landed on Veronica, and for a moment, she hesitated.

She cleared her throat. 'Remember, on this train, *everyone* has something to hide.'

The audience clapped.

Simone bowed, then strode toward Veronica.

'Well, well,' she said. 'Look what the casting couch dragged in. Tammy Doyle.'

Emily, the PA, sucked in a sharp breath, then buried her face in the show program. Zacky, still confused, frowned at Craig and mouthed *Tammy?* Paisley glanced at Aunt Mags. Aunt Mags chewed on her pen.

Veronica stared at Simone, a muscle working her jaw.

'It's Veronica,' she said. 'Chase. But you're still the same Simone. Still clinging to the fringes of the business. Still trotting out plays we did in college.' She clicked a long red nail on the show program.

Simone gave a stiff smile. 'Veronica. Yes. You did change your name. Why was that?' She tapped her chin. 'Oh, that's right. You dumped your husband, abandoned your baby, and booked it to Hollywood to steal a job that had been offered to your best friend. And who was that friend again? Oh, yes. Me.'

Veronica raised an eyebrow. 'Still bitter, I see.'

Simone shrugged. 'Not bitter. Clear-eyed. I'd rather be in my shoes tonight than yours. And Tony and Amber, wherever they are now, are better off without you.'

She turned and stalked away, leaving silence in her wake.

Malik brushed past. 'Lucky tonight's murder isn't real,' he murmured, 'or producer-lady would be leaving in a body bag.'

Tell me about it. But as dazed as we all were by the whole Tammy/Veronica/baby-dumping/job-stealing reveal, the show was about to begin.

I started to make my exit, then realized there was still a drink on my tray - a hurricane glass filled with something fizzy, a peach slice wedged on its rim.

I gave it an inconspicuous sniff.

Tangy. Fruity. Unless I was mistaken - and I wasn't - it was peach schnapps and Sprite. A slip of paper under the glass noted the seat number: 1.

I cut a glance at Seat 1. Had Veronica ordered this? I couldn't imagine it. A French 75 - maybe. A dirty martini - absolutely. But peach schnapps and Sprite?

Still, my job - as Veronica had pointed out - was to serve. I lifted the cocktail and, with a flourish, set it on the table before her.

She'd been half listening to Zacky drone on about himself. As she reached for her champagne, her gaze landed on the cocktail.

She went dead still. Then breathed one word: 'Tony.' Her eyes cut around the dining car.

I frowned. *Tony?*

'So did I mention I ran into Calvin Kessler?' Zacky was saying.

Veronica jerked her attention back to the conversation.

'Writer on *ClueQuest*,' Zacky explained to Paisley and Aunt Mags, like he was doing them a favor. 'Total meltdown during season five. Hasn't worked since.' He turned to Craig. 'Didn't you rep him?'

Craig swallowed a swig of champagne. 'I represented several

clients who didn't survive certain,' he cast a glance at Veronica, 'producers.'

Zacky nodded. 'Yeah, well, I ran into this one in detox. I mean, *I* wasn't detoxing, obviously. Just, you know, visiting. But yeah, guy looked rough, like, no-sleep, can't-afford-hair-product rough. Said he was working on a comeback. Some big blockbuster.'

'Interesting.' Veronica kept her voice casual, but held her champagne flute in a death grip. 'Did he say what this so-called blockbuster was?'

Zacky shook his head. 'You know how paranoid he always was. But hey! Is that where you got the idea for your show?'

Veronica froze. 'What?'

Zacky shrugged. 'His whole Maggie Smith fanboy thing. He was obsessed.'

Maggie Smith? From *Downton Abbey*? I narrowed my eyes.

'I assure you,' said Veronica, 'nothing Calvin did ever interested me, even when he worked for me.'

Her voice was measured, but small red specks began prickling her neck.

I glanced at my watch. And cleared my throat.

'Esteemed guests - and Zacky - enjoy your champagne. I will return momentarily with appetizers. In the meantime, if you need anything - refills, napkins, alibis, the name of a good lawyer', I raised a conspiratorial eyebrow, 'I'm but a discreet nod away.'

I gave a bow, then swayed back up the aisle, squeezing past the other actors who were taking their places for Act One.

As I approached the prep area, I stopped.

Anton stood in the shadow of the velvet curtain, rusty-blond hair sweat-plastered to his forehead, hand gripping his chef's knife. His eyes shot daggers across the car.

I followed his gaze. Unless I was mistaken - and I wasn't - those daggers were trained on Veronica.

Anton disappeared - back to his kingdom, no doubt - and I

slipped into the prep room to exchange my empty tray for the loaded serving cart.

A bell tinkled in the dining room. My cue. I wheeled the cart from behind the curtain, appetizer plates, whiskey glasses, and decanter of amber-colored water rattling on the top.

'Baxter. At last.' Malik, playing slacker son Reggie, sighed. 'We were starting to think you'd died.'

The dinner guests chuckled.

'What a tragedy that would be, sir,' I said, 'with no one left to pour your drinks.'

This time the guests full-out laughed. I even saw Veronica crack a thin smile.

Olivia Van Winter gave an obviously fake sniffle. 'Leland's here to read darling Alistair's will,' she sniffed.

'Indeed, madam. In which case, you'll need strength.' I held up the whiskey decanter, prompting more laughs.

I began serving the actors glasses of fake whiskey. Amelia Van Winter, loyal niece, primly set hers to the side, but Malik/Reggie snatched up the decanter as well.

'I need all the strength I can get,' he said.

Simone was working sound and lights at the tech console at the back, screened off from the guests. As Leland began reading the will, the lights flickered, and a howl of wind shuddered through the car, foreshadowing a snowstorm.

'Beloved and/or grudgingly tolerated family,' Leland intoned, 'I have prepared my last will and testament believing my firstborn, Alex Van Winter, lost to us these twenty years, is in fact dead. But should Alex prove to be alive, then Alex - and Alex alone - shall inherit the entirety of the Van Winter estate.'

The actors gasped, the lights flickered, and Act One came to a close.

I rolled my cart to the VIP table, where Zacky was already blathering.

'—so I told Craig.' He pitched his voice just loud enough to make sure the entire car could hear. 'I said, if Veronica's attached, I'm in. Didn't even need to read the script.'

Craig flashed a smooth, power-broker smile at Veronica. 'Admit it. Zac's got what you need - the jawline for period drama and the timing for criminal procedural.'

I froze, filigree bread basket halfway to the table.

They were talking about the role. *My* role.

The instant I'd read the logline in *Variety*—

It's *Downton Abbey* meets *CSI*: Upstairs, they're planning their next house party; downstairs, they're processing the crime scene.

—I'd stopped cold. In that moment, I knew: The part was mine. Veronica was convinced the show would skyrocket her career to the next level. I was counting on it to get mine off life support.

And now Zacky intended to take it.

I'd been standing, staring, too long, because Zacky clocked me and gave a smug smile.

'Ah, here to serve us again.' He glanced at my regally gloved hand, now unregally clenching the bread basket. 'Careful there Teddy - or is it Baxter? Don't want to damage the props. They'll have to take it out of your tips.' He cut his eyes toward Veronica for approval.

Weasel.

'Not to worry, sir.' I placed the bread on the table. 'The dinnerware will survive the evening. I cannot say the same for the guests.'

Zacky's face wrinkled in confusion. Paisley's shone in anticipation. Aunt Mags scribbled something in her notebook that Craig - covertly - tried to peek at. Emily slid a glance at Veronica, who gave me an appraising look.

The schnapps and Sprite still sat before her, the glass sweaty and untouched. She was, however, nursing the champagne. She took a sip as I lifted my tray from the cart.

'For your dining pleasure,' I said, 'Chef Anton—'

'*Kk—ahhk—!*' Veronica spit out a gasping cough.

Emily, in a panic, thrust a napkin toward her, which Veronica angrily swiped away.

She glared up at me. '*Anton?*'

'You're acquainted with our esteemed chef?' I said.

'Esteemed?' Veronica barked out a laugh that sounded like she was still choking. 'No.'

'Then let me introduce him by way of his signature dish.' I set appetizers before Zacky, then Craig. 'Pecan-stuffed dates, wrapped in bacon, with a honey glaze.'

'Bacon? Yes!' Zacky slid a date into his mouth and chewed blissfully.

Veronica studied him, eyes narrowed.

But when I set a plate before her, she turned on me.

'Pecans?' Her glare could've pierced steel. 'Are you *trying* to kill me? Surely you remember my nut allergy.'

Emily flashed her a startled look. I'm sure I did, too.

'My apologies.' I reached to retrieve the plate.

She waved me off, pushing the offending appetizer aside. 'Just serve the others.'

❧

'After everything I put up with.' Olivia Van Winter stormed down the aisle. 'I get nothing?'

Act Two had begun. I waited beside the VIP table for my cue.

'You?' said Reggie. 'I'm Father's only living child. And we're both out unless something happens to,' he and Olivia both turned toward Amelia, 'his niece.'

Amelia blinked innocently. 'I can't think *why* Uncle left his fortune to me. Unless it's because I nursed him through his long,

71

exhausting illness while you,' she looked at Reggie, 'gambled away your allowance, and you,' she turned to Olivia, 'took up tennis, or rather, your tennis instructor.'

Olivia sucked in a breath. 'Leland.' She placed a hand on the lawyer's sleeve. 'Can't you do something?'

Before Leland could answer, Cook scurried in. 'Sorry to interrupt, but I thought a bit of tea might be in order. I've set it out in the library with scones, including one of your favorites, Miss Amelia - raspberry.'

Beside me, Zacky had already wolfed down his appetizer. From the corner of my eye, I saw him eyeing Veronica's.

'You going to eat that?' he whispered.

Veronica rolled her eyes and pushed it toward him.

At that moment, the deep chime of a doorbell filled the dining car.

My cue.

I stepped forward.

'Apologies, Miss Van Winter. We have a guest.' I presented a calling card to Amelia.

She frowned at it. 'A.J. Grimley?'

'A reporter, whom I would've turned away if snow hadn't closed the roads.'

Amelia nodded. 'Where is this reporter now?'

'The library, miss.'

At that moment the train rattled into a long mountain tunnel, and Simone cut the lights.

The audience gasped.

In the pitch black, a cry rang out.

The lights sputtered on, and Paisley shot to her feet.

I expected her to clutch her throat and collapse.

Instead it was Zacky who lurched forward, clenching his chest, his face turning various shades of red.

Good grief. Somehow, he'd talked Paisley into letting him be the murder victim. He always did like to steal scenes.

He reached out, struggling to speak, then dropped face first onto the serving cart.

And milk them dry.

Amelia shrieked. Reggie fainted. Olivia clapped a hand over her mouth.

Paisley stared in disbelief.

I placed a hand on Zacky's back. 'Dead,' I said. 'The victim of a raspberry scone.'

⁂

The cast continued flinging insults and accusations. I exited, wheeling Zacky up the aisle. He was heavier than he looked, and when we finally rolled behind the velvet curtain, I stopped and sucked in air. I really needed to start working out.

'Okay, Zacky,' I breathed. 'Act's over. You can quit chewing the scenery.'

He didn't move.

'Zacky. We're backstage. It's okay to break character.'

Nothing.

'Zacky?'

I shook him. His arm dropped over the edge of the cart, and his head rolled to the side. His eyes stared up at me, lifeless and unblinking.

'Not. Funny.' I jabbed him - hard - in the ribs.

He didn't flinch.

I took a step back.

Okay.

Okay, I knew what to do. I'd been a detective, hadn't I?

Yeah - *on kids cable TV.* The only lifeless body Teddy Keene ever dealt with was a goldfish. And I couldn't very well flush Zacky.

But I could - *had to* - see if he was, well, alive.

I stretched a hand to feel his throat.

No beat. No pulse.

I pressed another spot.

Nothing.

'I can't *believe* he did that!'

I whirled.

Paisley Perez stood inside the curtain, hands on hips, quivering in fury.

'But—you—' I glanced at Zacky, then at Paisley. 'You can't be here.'

'No, I *should* be here. I won the tickets. I was supposed to be the dead body on the cart. That was the deal. And he—he—'

She flung an arm toward Zacky.

Then frowned. 'What's wrong with him?'

'Um, I think he's—' I couldn't say the word. 'I have to call 9-1-1.'

As I pulled my phone from my pocket, Paisley scrambled to Zacky's side.

I started to punch the number. 'You've got to be kidding.' I closed my eyes. 'No service.'

'We *are* going through a tunnel,' said Paisley, a bit breathlessly. 'In the Rockies. Where service is patchy anyway.'

I looked up. She'd turned Zacky onto his back and was now rhythmically pressing his chest with both hands.

I stared at her. 'You know CPR?'

'Well, yeah.' She continued pumping. 'There was a whole *ClueQuest* episode about it - The Code Blue Clue?'

Right. While she pressed, I checked his throat.

'Anything?' she asked.

I shook my head.

❧

We didn't have phone service. The police couldn't reach us till we arrived in Aspen anyway. And we didn't want the guests in a panic for the next hour, trapped on a train with, well, a dead guy.

So, I took his shoulders, Paisley took his feet, and we slid him into the narrow walk-in fridge. Paisley covered him with a tablecloth.

I leaned back against the fridge door—

—and spotted something brown and gooey on the floor.

A stuffed date, stickier and shinier than it should've been.

I picked it up with my waiter's cloth.

'You think he choked?' I said.

Paisley shook her head. 'It wasn't stuck in his throat. I checked. Maybe he was allergic, like Veronica.'

'And bolted down two helpings of something that could kill him?'

I gave it a sniff. It smelled sharp. Chemical. Like super-sweet fake sugar and . . . pepper.

'Vape juice,' I said. After *ClueQuest*, I'd gone to public school. I'd smelled a lot of liquid nicotine in my high school bathroom.

'Poison?' Paisley stared at me. 'But, who would want him dead?'

Well, there was . . . me. I mean, not really, but people might think so.

There was also—I looked up.

Paisley pulled back. '*I* didn't do it. I was mad he took your show, but if he hadn't, you wouldn't be working on this train, and I never would've met you.'

Okay. So. . .

My brain churned.

'It wasn't meant for him,' I said. 'He ate his own appetizer and was fine. He only collapsed after he ate Veronica's.'

Paisley considered this. 'No shortage of people who'd want *her* dead.'

'And still do,' I said.

She swallowed. 'We're stuck on a train with—'

'—a murderer.' I nodded. 'Who might try again.'

The actors filed into the prep area. Anton emerged from his lair with the main course. Paisley slipped away to take her seat.

This was the plan: Outwardly, we'd carry on like nothing happened. Secretly, Paisley would keep trying to call 9-1-1, and we'd both keep an eye on our suspects.

Simone had motive. Veronica stole her job and her career. But Simone hadn't gone near the appetizers.

Craig had means - he'd showed me his vape pen - and opportunity. His motive was weak, though. Veronica had fired past clients, but he was negotiating a deal with her now for Zacky (may he rest in peace).

Chef Anton had opportunity all over the place. But what was his motive? I'd seen him glaring at Veronica, but to be fair, he glared at everybody.

I rolled into the dining car to serve the prime rib, stealthily sniffing each plate before setting it out.

'Zacky's staying backstage,' Paisley was explaining. 'He's very method. He doesn't think it would look believable for the victim to come out and eat dinner.'

This victim especially.

As I set down the last plate, Amelia Van Winter swooned to the center of the car. Act Three had begun.

'The scone was meant for me! Someone tried,' Amelia gulped, 'to kill me.'

Reggie nodded. 'We're snowed in, so the killer's still here. It's one of us.'

'You, me, or Leland,' said Olivia.

'Or the staff,' Leland pointed out. 'Baxter or Cook.'

I took a breath. Time to implement the next part of the plan: Get the entire dining car to watch Veronica so no one could murder her.

I cleared my throat. 'Apologies, but I believe you've forgotten someone.'

The cast turned, puzzled. Dinner train players expected improvisation, but they were clearly surprised.

'Veronica Chase.' I motioned toward her. 'Mr. Carrington's legal assistant. She's been here all evening, but with her mild, unassuming nature,' yes, I nearly choked on the words 'she's easily overlooked.'

The cast shot each other confused looks.

Veronica stared at me, open-mouthed. Then smiled. She was, as I'd expected, flattered to be pulled into the spotlight.

'That's right, I have.' She stood. 'And I've seen everything.'

Wow. She'd plunged right in. I might have created a monster.

As the cast performed, accusing each other, defending themselves, ad-libbing with Veronica, I was struck by the parallels between the play and the actual murder.

The play characters were snowed in at a mansion. We were trapped on a train.

The play victim died by poisoned scone, Zacky by poisoned date.

In both, it seemed the wrong person had been murdered.

And Baxter the butler held the first clue.

'Pardon me.' I stepped forward. 'But I took the liberty of checking our unfortunate visitor's pockets.' I held up a wallet. 'It seems A.J. Grimley was in fact—'

Simone's dramatic organ chords swelled.

'—Alex Van Winter.'

Both cast and audience gasped.

I watched Veronica. She was loving this. Her eyes sparkled. Her neck flushed.

And something niggled my brain.

I studied Veronica's flush, then Emily's blotches, redder than her coppery hair.

And it clicked.

I stepped toward Emily. 'Enjoying yourself, Miss Amber?' I murmured.

She looked up, started to smile, then froze. She cut a glance at Veronica.

I raised my eyebrows. 'She doesn't know?'

Emily/Amber shook her head. 'I just,' she swallowed, 'wanted to get close.'

'Of course,' I said sympathetically.

I moved toward Paisley.

'Emily,' I whispered, 'is Amber.'

Paisley's eyes grew wide.

We had a new suspect. One with motive and opportunity.

And I was pretty sure I'd uncovered the motive of another.

&

Backstage, Anton was prepping dessert. His rusty hair, very similar to Emily/Amber's, peeked out beneath his skullcap.

I set the untouched hurricane glass beside him. 'Sorry, Tony. She didn't like it.'

He glanced at it. And shrugged. 'People change.'

'Is that what you want?' I said. 'Revenge for everything she changed?'

He leveled a look at me. 'What I want,' he said, 'is to plate dessert. And keep my daughter safe.'

&

I wheeled my cart, weighed down with cherries and brandy, to my table. Paisley caught my eye, waved her phone, and gave a thumbs up. She'd reached 9-1-1.

To stay on schedule, we always played the final scene during dessert.

'The reporter was actually my brother?' Reggie/Malik, at the next table, uncorked his brandy. 'If only I'd known.'

Veronica narrowed her eyes. 'Are you sure you didn't?'

I had to admit, she fit right in. Almost like she was supposed to be there.

Of course, she knew the play. Simone said they'd done it in college.

I stopped.

She knew the play.

She knew the poison wasn't meant for Amanda Van Winter. It was meant for the character who actually died. Amanda made sure of it, to hold onto the Van Winter fortune.

As I opened my brandy, I scrolled through everything that had happened: Veronica's project, Simone's stolen job, Zacky meeting Calvin Kessler. And it all fell into place.

'But Reggie *wasn't* the one who knew,' I cried out.

The cast let out a collective sigh. I was going annoyingly off-script again.

Still, I brandished the brandy. 'You may not be aware, but Veronica Chase is actually a Hollywood producer.'

The guests murmured.

Veronica gave a humble smile.

I poured brandy onto the cherries.

'She disguised herself as a mild-mannered assistant to secretly follow A.J. Grimley, a.k.a. Zacky Templeton.'

Veronica cut me a look.

I pulled out a long-handled lighter.

'You see, Zacky stumbled onto information that proved Veronica stole the idea for her blockbuster show.'

Veronica narrowed her eyes.

I clicked the lighter.

'Poor Zacky had no idea what it meant, but if it came out, it would ruin her. And so Veronica Chase—'

I lit the cherries. *Whoooooosh.* Flames shot into the air.

'—murdered him.'

The audience erupted in applause.

I took a bow. I'd solved the mystery - and flambéd my career.

It was after midnight before Aspen P.D. let us off the train.

Paisley, Aunt Mags, Malik, and I stood on the platform, watching detectives lead Veronica away.

Malik bumped my shoulder. 'It was always going to be a long shot.'

I nodded.

I turned to Paisley and Aunt Mags. 'I'm sorry your big winning night was such a bust.'

'Are you kidding?' Paisley stared at me, eyes wide. 'I solved a mystery with Teddy Blake.'

'And you both performed brilliantly.' Aunt Mags slid her notebook into her handbag. 'You've given me an idea for my next novel.'

'Novel?' I frowned.

Paisley nodded. 'I told you Aunt Mags was big into mysteries.'

Variety - Teddy Blake, formerly of TV's *ClueQuest*, has inked a deal to star in the adaptation of bestselling novelist Mags Perez's blockbuster mystery, *Murder on the Dinner Train Express*, in a reported eight-figure payday brokered by newly minted associate agent Paisley Perez of the Craig Loomis Talent Group.

BIO:

When Lisa Knudsen Harkrader was in third grade, she wanted to be a writer, an artist, and a spy. Today, she's a writer and illustrator who has published forty-five books for children, has received the William Allen White Children's Book Award and four Kansas Notable Book awards, and has been on children's choice award lists in eight states. And she still wants to be a spy.

RECIPE

Pecan-stuffed Dates Wrapped in Bacon with Honey Glaze

This delicious appetizer is incredibly easy and requires only four ingredients.

Note: *Poison is not a recommended ingredient. It ruins the flavor, endangers the guests, and annoys the household staff.*

Ingredients
8 slices bacon
16 pitted dates
16 pecan halves
1 tablespoon honey

Equipment
16 toothpicks
Baking sheet
Parchment paper or nonstick cooking spray

Method
Preheat oven to 400° F.
Stuff each date with a pecan.
Cut bacon slices in half. Wrap each date with a half slice of bacon and secure with a toothpick.
Place bacon-wrapped dates on a baking sheet sprayed with nonstick cooking spray or lined with parchment paper.
Bake 15–20 minutes, until bacon is desired crispiness.
Brush dates with honey.
Serve warm.

Chapter Five

A PINCH OF POISON

Marti M. McNair

When a revered resident at a Highland care home dies under suspicious circumstances, siblings Iona and Harris are drawn into a mystery steeped in secrets, grudges, and foxglove. With roads closed and time ticking, they must unravel the truth - because in Glenheath House, even tranquillity hides a bitter dose of revenge.

Nestled deep within the heather-cloaked folds of the Highland glen, Glenheath House sat like an ageing laird. Its frame, stooped and timeworn, rested amid a velvet cushion of lilac heather. The house, though weathered, exuded a quiet, enduring dignity. Ancient Scots pines stood guard around its crooked chimneys; the tree's needles whispered secrets into the wind that swept in off the loch. Moss crept over stone walls, and a low mist curled along the gravel path as if mystical sleeping creatures exhaled their breath.

In the garden, roses wrestled with wild thistle, and the old sundial kept time not by sunlight, but by the rhythm of tea rounds and tartan blankets. It was the sort of place where the air carried the scent of peat and woodsmoke, and where the stories of times long past clung to the soil. The mountains loomed above, watching with ancient, knowing eyes.

The crunch of tyres on the gravel broke the peace as a battered blue Land Rover pulled up beside the low stone wall. Iona Maclean stepped out first, the Highland breeze tugging playfully at her scarf, her copper curls breaking free. Her brother Harris followed, taller, quieter, his sharp eyes scanning the crooked gables and ivy-clad windows.

They paused, taking it all in. The smell of pine and damp earth, the distant caw of crows, and the brooding presence of the bens beyond. Glenheath wasn't just a care home to them. It was where their Great Grandad Mac waited patiently for their monthly visit.

Inside, the familiar warmth embraced them, warding off the cold. The familiar, strong aroma of lavender polish and the faint medicinal tang of antiseptic greeted them. The corridors were lined with faded photographs of Highland games and ceilidhs. Tartan curtains framed windows looking out into bramble-fringed paths.

Behind the great oak reception desk sat Morag MacPherson, her thick grey bun pinned like a crown and her wool cardigan buttoned right to her throat. She glanced up from her magazine with a bright smile and nodded towards the visitors' book. 'Lovely to see you, dears . . . my, how time has flown by since your last visit. Your great-grandfather's in the dining room having a bit of lunch. He's been fair excited for ye' coming . . . could hardly sit still this morning. His mood's been a bit down recently, saying nothing ever happens around here. No excitement at all.'

Iona and Harris both nodded politely, but it was Iona who spoke. 'Thank you, Morag. It's good to be back. Stepping into the Highlands . . . it's like stepping into a different world. So peaceful and beautiful. I don't know why Gramps could ever be feeling down.'

'You're lucky you made it through when you did. I was listening to the radio and there's been another landslide up at the Rest and Be Thankful,' Morag said. 'The road's closed now because rocks the size of sheep tumbled down. They say it'll take hours to clear.'

❦

Gramps raised a liver-spotted hand in greeting. 'Hello, lovelies. Great to see you.' His voice was warm, and his smile deepened the creases on his weather-beaten face. A tartan rug lay folded across his knees, and his walking stick rested against the back of his chair.

Iona leaned in to kiss his cheek while Harris pulled up a chair beside him, brushing crumbs off the floral seat cushion before sitting. The dining room was filled with soft clatter - teacups meeting saucers, the scrape of cutlery, and the gentle hum of conversation rolling around.

'Chef's done a shepherd's pie again,' Gramps said, with a theatrical sigh. 'Same as Thursday . . . and last Thursday . . . and the Thursday before that. Tastes like regret and boiled hope.'

Iona stifled a laugh. 'I'm sure it's not that bad.'

'Oh, it is,' Harris murmured, eyeing a plate as it passed, the mince grey and lifeless beneath a lumpy mash topping.

At the far end of the room, Lord Alastair Cairncross sat alone at his table, stiff-backed and sharp-eyed despite his years. A gold watch glinted on his wrist as he raised his fork. A hush rippled through the nearby tables. Even in retirement, Cairncross carried the air of authority. He was polished, cold, and impossible to ignore.

'He looks grumpier than usual,' Gramps muttered. 'Probably because Nurse Doyle didn't slip him a nip of whisky with his medicine.'

As if on cue, Nurse Doyle swept past, her features tight and her steps clipped. Behind her, Chef Archie emerged from the kitchen, red-faced and muttering, wiping his hands on a grease-stained apron. Then, a sharp gasp, a rattle of crockery and Lord Cairncross clutched his throat, his eyes wide. His chair scraped as he lurched forward, knocking his spoon to the floor. For a heartbeat, the room froze. Then, Mable McTavish screamed.

Harris was on his feet in an instant, pushing past a stunned resident clutching her napkin to her mouth. Iona followed close behind, weaving through the growing circle of onlookers. Lord Cairncross lay slumped over the table.

Nurse Doyle appeared, breathless and flushed, and dropped to her knees beside him. She snapped the words over her shoulder. 'Call for an ambulance. Now.'

'It won't get through,' Archie said. 'The road is closed.'

Iona's gaze found her brothers. 'What just happened?'

'He choked,' Harris said, keeping his voice low. 'I guess whatever he had with his custard was too lumpy.'

Gramps, still seated, leaned closer. 'That wasn't choking. That man was poisoned.'

Iona blinked. 'What makes you say that?'

Gramps gave a wary shrug. 'Lived long enough to know the look of someone who's been silenced . . . and believe me, Alistair Cairncross made enough enemies to fill Loch Ness.'

Across the room, Archie stood frozen in the kitchen door-way, his face turning pale. Nurse Doyle knelt motionless by the lifeless body, her jaw tight. Outside the dining room window, the gardener, Gregor, stared in, unmoving, hands still clutching a tray of seedlings.

Harris glanced at Iona. 'Peaceful Highland visit, eh?'

❧

The residents were herded into the day room - muttering, hugging, clutching cardigans tightly as if the wool alone could ward off whatever had just happened. The room smelled of barley sugars and sweet cinnamon. A battered upright piano sat in the corner beside a tweed sofa, and the television buzzed low with the sound turned down.

'Poor Lord Cairncross,' muttered Mrs MacKinnon, a retired headmistress with a fondness for gin and speculation. 'Mind you, he wasn't exactly a ray of sunshine. Always correcting folk. Once told me my Gaelic pronunciation was borderline criminal. And I taught languages for thirty years.'

'Aye,' said Mr Lafferty, who wore three jumpers and read nothing but the *Daily Record.* 'Wouldnae be surprised if someone finally snapped. The man was the kind who made enemies with a handshake. You all know what happened back in the day.'

In the corner, Morag wrung her hands behind the tea trol-ley, whispering fiercely to Gregor who, for some reason, was now in the dining room. He shifted from foot to foot, eyes fixed on the carpet, his hands still grubby with soil, and a smear of compost clinging to one sleeve. 'I wasn't even in the kitchen,' he hissed. 'I was repotting the geraniums . . . ask Archie.'

Archie was pacing the room, red-faced and scowling. 'Don't drag me into it, Gregor. Everyone's always blaming the cook when something goes wrong. It's not like I poured rat poison in the gravy.'

'Bit defensive, isn't he?' Harris murmured, his eyes following Archie's twitchy movements.

Iona nodded, watching as Nurse Doyle perched on the window ledge, her arms folded over her chest. Her lips were pressed thin as she stared into the distance.

'She hated Cairncross,' Iona whispered. 'Gramps said they argued nearly every week about his medication and how he always refused her help.'

'And don't forget Mrs Malcolm,' Harris added, nodding towards a steely-eyed woman in a mauve cashmere sweater. 'She and Cairncross used to bicker about politics over every single meal. She once called him a relic of imperial rot . . . loud enough for the whole dining hall to hear.'

Iona tilted her head, her mind already ticking. 'Let's say someone had a reason to want him gone. Nurse Doyle would've had access to his meds. Gregor could've slipped something into the herbs he grows for the kitchen. Archie's meals are always under fire. Or . . .'

'Or Morag,' Harris added. 'Knows everyone's comings and goings. Knows who's visiting, when deliveries arrive . . .'

They both fell silent as Gramps limped in, still alert despite the shock. 'Start with the food,' he said, without preamble. 'No one dies like that from indigestion. It will be a while before the police arrive. Every second in any investigation counts.'

'Gramps,' Iona whispered, 'We're not exactly detectives.'

'You're Highlanders. That's good enough for me,' Gramps replied. 'Besides, with the road closure it will take a while before anyone reaches us.'

Iona and Harris exchanged a glance as they moved through the day room, careful not to look like they were prying, simply concerned, attentive great-grandchildren passing the time. But behind every polite smile, their eyes were alert, watching for signs of guilt in every darted glance.

Mrs Malcolm, seated by the radiator with a mug of weak tea, was the first to speak without prompting. 'Well, I'm just saying,' she muttered, as they approached her, 'If you spend your life making enemies, you can't be shocked when one comes knocking.'

'You knew Lord Cairncross well?' Iona asked, with a sad smile.

'Knew of him,' Mrs Rutherford said, then sniffed. 'We didn't see eye to eye, let's leave it at that. Just last week, he called me a bleeding-heart radical. I said he was a fantasist – thinking we still lived in the empire. He made a hobby of being disliked.'

Harris raised a brow. 'Any idea who might've disliked him enough to do something drastic?'

She leaned in, her voice a murmur. 'I saw Nurse Doyle emptying his pill box yesterday, muttering under her breath. I don't trust that one. She runs this place as if we're all fruit loops rather than pensioners.'

They thanked her and drifted on, toward Morag, who was now dishing out chocolate biscuits on a fancy tray as if they were peace offerings.

'Strange day, isn't it?' Iona said.

Morag sighed. 'I always said something like this would happen to Lord Cairncross eventually.'

'Why's that?' Harris asked.

Morag looked around before answering. 'Alistair Cairncross wasn't just a politician back in the day. He had business interests. Money in all sorts of shady pots, if rumour's to be believed. He caused many a person around this area a great deal of heartache. And if you ask him about it, he doesn't seem to care. He's had lots of threats from all sorts of people over the years.'

'Threats,' Iona repeated.

Morag nodded. 'Anonymous threats. He told Nurse Doyle that people wanted him to answer for his past. Nurse Doyle wanted him to report the threats to the police. But he wouldn't hear of it.'

Iona and Harris stole a glance across the room to where

Nurse Doyle sat stiffly, her hands clenched in her lap. They wandered over, and she looked up, eyes red-rimmed.

'You'll be thinking it was me, all my fault. That I gave him the wrong medication,' she said, bluntly. 'I didn't.'

'We didn't think that at all,' Iona replied.

'He was a nightmare. Refused his blood pressure tablets, and hid his warfarin,' Nurse Doyle said. 'I didn't poison him. I just wanted him to take what the doctors prescribed without him accusing me of being part of some MI5 conspiracy. He accused me of all sorts at times.'

'Did he have enemies here?'

She gave a dry laugh. 'He had enemies everywhere. I don't think I ever came across anyone who said anything nice about him.'

'Morag told us about people making threats. What can you tell us about that?'

'I shouldn't really say too much as it's confidential. But he has a pile of letters in his drawer. Most of them are begging letters from his family. Some are from way back when he was a politician – when he made choices that affected people's livelihoods. However, he accused me of slipping an untoward note under his door. That he'd be watching me. I told him he needed to speak with the police if he thought he was at risk. But he wouldn't hear of it.'

Across the room, Chef Archie was still muttering under his breath, wiping beads of sweat from his forehead with a dishcloth.

'He's still acting odd,' Harris said.

Iona nodded. 'We need to talk to him. And Gregor too.'

Before they could make a move, Mr Lafferty beckoned them over. 'Don't waste your time with the cook. It's always the quiet ones you have to watch. That gardener spends more time loitering and talking to his plants than doing anything useful. Mind you, his plants could probably make more sense out of him than any of us in here.'

Gregor, standing nearby with a tray of tea, heard him. 'And you spend more time stirring trouble than sipping your tea, Lafferty,' he said, shooting him with a dark look. 'What were you doing wandering around the kitchen just before Cairncross's meal was served?'

Morag snapped. 'Enough. This is a care home, not a courtroom.'

But it was too late. The seed had been sown. Accusations began to bubble beneath the surface. Every sideways glance, every whispered comment, added weight to the growing tension. Not one person in the nursing home was safe from suspicion.

Iona and Harris slipped out of the day room. The chatter and accusations faded behind them as they crossed the corridor and stepped back into the dining room. The chairs were still askew, plates half-cleared, and a faint aroma of stewed mince still hung in the air.

Iona's gaze drifted to Lord Cairncross, now resting on the floor, shrouded beneath a long white tablecloth, awaiting the forensic team. The spoon lay where it had fallen, his custard untouched. 'Somewhere between pudding and poison,' she murmured. 'That's where the truth is hiding.'

Harris nodded. 'Let's start from where the food came from.'

They pushed through the double doors into the kitchen. Pots soaked in sinks, and a fan rattled overhead. A clipboard hung by the pantry with menus scribbled in faded ink. Harris scanned it. 'Shepherd's pie. Custard and toffee sponge. Tea with one sugar for Cairncross. Nothing fancy,' he said. 'But all of it came through here.'

Iona opened a large store cupboard to find herb pots - parsley, thyme, and a struggling basil plant near the back. 'Gregor grows these. Maybe something suspicious was fed to the herbs.'

'Bit risky, though,' Harris said, checking a tin of custard for tampering. 'Too many variables. You'd need to be sure the poison would reach the right person.'

'Or,' Iona said, her eyes narrowing. 'You'd know exactly what he eats, drinks, and when.'

A small, empty glass sat on the draining board. Harris picked it up and held it to his nose. A rich, warming scent clung to the rim. Something sharp and spiced, with a trace of oak and burnt sugar. He frowned. 'Whatever this was, it smells expensive,' he muttered.

They exchanged a glance, wondering where to go next. 'Let's check out the potting shed,' Harris suggested.

They stepped out the back door and into the soft grey drizzle. The garden unfolded before them, prim and orderly. Rose bushes tentatively budded, vegetable beds bordered by mossy sleepers, and, near the tree line, a weathered potting shed.

'So, this is Gregor's domain,' Harris said, as they entered.

A pair of shears hung from a hook, and pots of herbs sat half-watered on a bench. 'Foxglove,' Iona said, pointing to a plant tucked behind the rosemary. 'Beautiful but deadly.'

Harris frowned. 'Why would a deadly plant like that be in here?'

'That's something we need to find out,' Iona replied.

Other than the Foxglove, the shed revealed nothing more than spades, compost bags and a few pairs of muddy wellies. Still, something itched at the back of Iona's mind. She couldn't quite put her finger on what she was trying to remember. She turned on her heels. 'Come on. Let's see Cairncross's room.'

The room sat on the second floor, overlooking the east lawn. Iona and Harris stepped inside, their footsteps muffled by the threadbare carpet. They crossed to where the writing desk sat nestled beneath the window. 'Here,' Iona said, giving the stubborn drawer a firm tug.

Inside, a neat stack of papers lay. Letters. Some typed and

some handwritten. The top one had no name, only a line - *You think that time will protect you. It won't.*

Harris picked up a second, his eyebrows lifting. 'Looks as if someone stood on this one, it has a footprint on it.'

'Perhaps it was the one slipped under his door,' Iona said, taking the note from Harris and reading the scribbled handwriting. She took in a huge breath. 'Someone definitely had a grudge.'

They placed the letters back where they had found them, apart from the one with the footprint mark. Harris slipped that note into his jeans pocket.

❧

Back downstairs, the day room was quieter - the crowd having thinned out somewhat. Nurse Doyle remained by the window, a lukewarm cup of tea untouched in her hand. The siblings ambled over, and suddenly, the source of the nagging feeling Iona had in the potting shed became clear.

'Nurse Doyle,' Iona began, rubbing a hand over her chin. 'Did Lord Cairncross have any heart problems?'

She looked guarded. 'He did. Atrial fibrillation. We managed it.'

'Was he prescribed anything herbal?' Iona asked. 'Something derived from foxglove, maybe?'

Nurse Doyle thought for a second. 'Digoxin. It's based on foxglove, yes. But it was in tablet form and strictly regulated. We have records. And he hadn't had a dose for two days. He refused it. He said it made him feel - tethered.' Her face twisted. 'He accused me of trying to slow him down.'

'Could anyone else have slipped him some? Perhaps something more concentrated?'

'Only if they knew what they were doing,' she said, setting the cup down. 'A few leaves in a stew could stop a heart.' Her gaze shifted between Gregor and Archie. 'It would take someone reckless or experienced. However, it was only Lord Cairncross who was poisoned.'

。

Later that afternoon, while the residents dozed or played some cards, Harris and Iona returned to reception, to the small admin alcove beside the desk. The visitor's log sat open, pages curled at the corners. Iona ran a finger down the margins until she found it, a quick note in blue ink – *Reminder: check dressing stock - M*. The handwriting was slanted with bold looped capitals.

Harris pulled the note from his pocket and held it against the visitors' log. 'No mistaking it. It's the same handwriting.'

'Morag,' Iona whispered. 'She wrote this.'

。

Iona and Harris sat in Morag's small, cluttered office. Iona pushed the note across the desk, towards her. 'Did you slip this under Lord Cairncross's bedroom door?'

Morag sat in her chair, elbows on the desk with her hands clasped tightly. A bead of sweat slipped down her temple. Her mouth fell open. 'Yes . . . but I didn't mean . . . I didn't mean I was going to poison him.'

Harris pushed himself up from the chair. He crossed to Morag's side of the desk, his eyes falling on the note, 'If you don't change your ways, your time here at the home will end sooner than you think. Next time someone offers you a cuppa, sniff it like a bloodhound at a crime scene.' He let the final words hang in the air.

Morag inhaled deeply. 'It was only to scare him. He was so mean to everyone – especially Mr Lafferty.'

Iona chewed on her bottom lip. 'Morag, did you put a nip of Foxglove in Lord Cairncross's tea?'

'No. Absolutely not.'

'Did you lace his custard with it?' Iona asked, one eyebrow cocked.

Morag managed a half smile. 'If that's what you think, lock me up in here until the police come. I'm sure they'll get to the bottom of this.' She opened the bottom drawer of her desk, producing a bottle of red wine and a chipped floral mug. She set both on the desk, then sank back into her chair. 'Might as well make myself comfortable,' she said, twisting the screw top. 'Do you fancy a drop? I'm not a wine snob - but if you're after something less tragic than this mug, there's a cupboard full of glasses in the kitchen.'

☙

Iona and Harris found Chef Archie sat slouched in a vinyl armchair. He saw them coming and stiffened.

'I thought we could pick your brain, Archie,' Iona said.

'Better than my pockets, I suppose,' Archie replied.

'Or your pantry,' Harris added.

'If this is about Cairncross,' Archie said, his face falling. 'I've said it before and I'll say it again, my shepherd's pie might offend a critic, but it's not fatal. Not unless you've got a deep-seated allergy to personality.'

'Humour us,' Iona said, smiling. 'What exactly goes into your famous shepherd's pie?'

Archie brightened, as if someone had switched him to show-off mode. 'Right, first, you take minced lamb – fresh, if you can get it. Brown it in a pan until it confesses all its sins. Then chuck in onions, garlic, and whatever root veg you can get your hands on. Add a splash of red wine . . .' He stopped, blinking twice.

'What is it?' Iona asked.

'Nothing. Well, I don't think it's nothing. Anyway, where was I?'

'Mash,' Harris said. 'I think you were at the part where you needed to add the mash.'

'Ah yes. Potatoes, boiled till they surrender, mash them up with plenty of butter, a splash of milk, and a pinch of something. I sometimes use crushed roast crisps for texture.'

Iona screwed her face. 'Crisps.'

'I call it my crunch of danger.' He stopped again. 'You don't think it was me who poisoned Cairncross? As much as I didn't like the man, I would never cause him harm.'

&

They found Gregor lurking by the French doors in the family visiting room, half-concealed behind a drooping rubber plant, his gardening gloves dangling from his back pocket.

Harris cleared his throat, and Gregor flinched.

'We just had a word with Archie,' Iona said, reaching out and touching the rubber plant's leaves. It felt cool and waxy. 'Thought we'd have a quick chat with you too.'

Gregor shuffled, and Iona noticed his eyes flickering toward the hedge line in the garden outside. Was he plotting to make a dash for it?

'I didn't touch or tamper with the food,' he muttered. 'I grow rosemary, not resentment.'

'Foxglove too,' Harris said.

The coloured drained from Gregor's face. 'It's ornamental.'

'Did you see anyone hanging around your potting shed lately?

He hesitated. 'Lafferty strolled down yesterday. Asked me if valerian could help him sleep.'

'Valerian?' Harris asked.

Iona nodded. 'It's a herbal plant, known for its mild sedative properties.'

Gregor looked impressed. 'You know your stuff.'

'Did you manage to help him out?' Harris asked Gregor.

Gregor shook his head. 'I told him to try some whisky instead.'

Iona gave him a long look. 'Could Mr Lafferty have noticed the Foxglove?

Gregor's jaw twitched. 'The residents and staff wander through the gardens here. No where is out of bounds. But I don't think any of them would know the difference between parsley and poison. And most folk here think thyme's what you put in clocks.'

Archie stood in the doorway of the lounge, arms folded, and his eyes narrowing like a man halfway remembering something important.

'Are you okay?' Harris asked.

'I didn't add the wine,' he said, staring at Iona. 'The wine always gives the pie a splash of soul. Morag told me we were out. Said the delivery was delayed and the cellar was bone dry. So, I used beef stock and an old flavouring cube instead.' He scratched his head. 'But it wasn't a flavouring cube I made. It was just something I found in the cupboard.'

'I don't believe it was anything you put in the food,' Iona said, resting a comforting hand on Archie's shoulder. 'It must have been something given specifically to Lord Cairncross, as everyone else who ate dinner is perfectly fine.'

Iona's brow furrowed as she glanced at Harris. 'Let's head back up to Cairncross's room. I swear the answer is hiding in those letters. Somewhere.'

They trudged back up the creaking staircase. The room felt colder now, as though Cairncross's ghost lingered, eyes watching from the shadows. Harris pulled the drawer open. 'Here, you take this pile,' he said, handing a bunch of letters to his sister as they dropped to the floor, spreading them out.

Iona's eyes narrowed as she sifted through them yanking out every note bearing the same looping handwriting. 'Well, well,' she muttered. 'Our Morag has been quite the prolific pen pal.'

Harris pushed himself up from the floor. 'I wonder what else is hiding in these drawers,' he said, yanking one open. Paper crinkled as he rummaged through a tangle of handkerchiefs and dusty trinkets. 'Hey, Iona,' he said, his fingers closing around a yellowed newspaper clipping. 'Take a look at this.' The headline screamed in bold black letters *"Young Politician Oversees Closure of Lafferty Linen Group."*

The accompanying photograph captured a moment frozen in time - a younger, cocky Cairncross, his dark hair as thick as his ego. He was oblivious to the fury blazing in the factory owner's eyes. The man's jaw clenched tight, his fist half-raised as though he was seconds away from launching a punch. Beside them, a waif of a girl clung to her father's side, her eyes wide and haunted.

Iona whistled, leaning in closer. 'I think we should gather everyone in the dayroom.'

Gramps sent word for everyone to return to the large lounge, his voice carrying through the corridors like a town crier's bell. When the murmur of speculation finally settled, Iona stepped forward, her gaze sweeping the room. 'Thank you all for your patience,' she said, her voice loud for those hard of hearing. 'We're still piecing together what happened to Lord Cairncross. Hopefully, the road will clear soon, and the police can take over.'

A collective sigh of relief rippled through the room. Harris took his place beside his sister, his eyes fixing on Mr Lafferty. 'Mr Lafferty,' he began. 'Are you any relation to the Lafferty family that owned the Lafferty Linnen Group - the one that Cairncross oversaw the closure of back in . . . ?'

Before Harris could finish, Mr Lafferty's fists balled in his lap. 'Aye, that was a bitter pill to swallow,' he said, his tone gruff. 'My older brother owned the mill. Cairncross shut it down, putting hundreds out of work. Families torn apart. My brother never recovered. Died not long after. His wife, Betty, moved away and remarried. We lost touch.'

'I'm sorry to hear this,' Iona said.

Lafferty's brow creased. 'But everyone knows that piece of history. Cairncross and I hated each other. If I was going to poison him, I'd have done it years ago.'

Iona retrieved the crumpled newspaper clipping from her jacket pocket. She approached Morag whose lips were cherry red from the wine she had supped. 'Is this you as a child, Morag? Was your maiden name Lafferty?'

Morag's hand shot to her mouth. 'I don't know what you're on about. I've never been married.' She pointed to the picture. 'That photo's so blurred, the child could be anyone.'

Iona shook her head. 'We've examined all the letters, and some are from years ago – long before you started working here at the home. When the receptionist and caretaker positions became available, I believe you saw it as an opportunity to settle a score.'

Mr Lafferty rose from his chair, and with a slow shuffle, he hobbled across the room. Reaching Morag, he took her hands in his, his gnarled fingers trembling slightly. He studied her face for a moment, his eyes widening. Recognition dawned. 'Well, I never,' he muttered, his voice laced with disbelief. 'Morag . . . it's really you.' A stunned pause followed before he leaned in closer, peering into her eyes. 'Why did I not see the likeness sooner? You should've told me who you were - told me it was you. I'm your uncle. Is that why you always treated me better than the other residents?' He thought for a moment. 'Now that I come to think of it, Betty's new husband was a MacPherson.'

Morag gasped, her voice quivering. 'I didn't mean to kill him. I just wanted him to suffer a little, but the dose of Foxglove I slipped into his brandy must have been too strong.'

Harris shot Iona a knowing look. 'The empty glass on the draining board. It was brandy I smelled.' He turned to Morag. 'Did you lift the glass during the commotion?'

Tears welled in Morag's eyes. 'Yes, I rinsed it out. I was trying to hide the evidence. You have to believe me. I didn't think the Foxglove would be so potent.'

❦

A few hours later, Detective Inspector McDonald arrived with the paramedics. They took over the scene, jotting down notes and quietly conferring as they pieced together the afternoon's peculiar events.

Back in Gramps's room, Iona and Harris, and Gramps huddled together with mugs of hot chocolate and thick slices of vanilla sponge.

'At least all this poison malarkey hasn't put me off my food,' Gramps said, chewing a large mouthful. 'Archie's shepherd's pie might be questionable, but the man knows his way around a cake tin.'

'You do realise it was Morag who sabotaged his efforts,' Iona said, wiping crumbs from her knees. 'She took the last bottle of wine.'

Harris looked over at her thoughtfully. 'Maybe she knew she'd be caught. And in some strange way, she was celebrating her success.'

Iona stared into her cup. The sweetness of the chocolate clung to her lips, but her heart felt heavy. 'I feel sorry for her,' she said quietly.

Outside, the Highland wind stirred the heather, carrying with it the scent of rain. And once more, Glenheath House settled into its usual tranquillity - where, officially at least, nothing ever happened.

BIO:

Having had a passion for reading and writing since an early age, this passion has only grown over the years. Marti M. Mcnair has been writing since she could pick up a pen and after her children flew the nest she turned to writing seriously. Her main focus is writing for a YA audience, and her books feature dystopian settings, dark political undercurrents and places her characters in precarious situations which tests them to the limit. She was the winner of the prestigious Scottish Association of Writers, Barbara Hammond Prize. She is also a partner in Auscot Publishing and retreats and a graphic designer for Writers' narrative eMagazine.

RECIPE

Shepherd's Pie
A dish best served warm - unlike Lord Cairncross.
Serves - One cantankerous nobleman and a room full of suspects. Prep time - However long it takes to locate the poison. Cook time - Until the alibi's firm.

Ingredients
500g minced lamb (shepherd's choice - possibly stolen from a rival glen.)
1 onion, finely chopped (or viciously hacked - we're not judging.)
2 carrots (to appear wholesome.)
A suspicious amount of fresh herbs (bonus points if grown by a man named Gregor.)
A splash of red wine (pour yourself a glass while you're at it.)
1 teaspoon tomato purée (or blood of thine enemies.)

1 stock cube (or something that looks like a stock cube.)
A pinch of salt.
A pinch of poison (optional, but popular at Glenheath House.)
1 heap of mashed potatoes (fluffy enough to smother a scandal.)

Method

Interrogate your ingredients. If they refuse to talk, chop them finely and threaten to add them to Nurse Doyle's patient tray. In a large pan, fry the onion until translucent, like the lies told at afternoon tea. Brown the mince as if it's holding onto secrets. Stir in carrots, herbs, and a stock cube - just make sure it's not that foxglove cube you keep for emergencies.
Add wine (if Morag hasn't hoarded it in her desk drawer). Let the ingredients bubble while you ponder your motives. Bring to a simmer - until the mixture looks thick and suspiciously hearty. Pour it into a casserole dish like it's a confession. Cover with a generous layer of mashed potato, spread with care - or contempt. Optional - sculpt a message in Morse code to the coroner. Bake at 180°C until golden brown, with just a hint of moral ambiguity.

To Serve

Garnish with parsley, suspicion, and a side of whispered accusations. Ideal for stormy Highland afternoons when murder is in the air and the road is closed.

Chef's Tip

If everyone else survives the meal, don't panic - the poison might just be slow-release. Or the wrong person ate it. Best to keep a sherry decanter and your conscience close.

Chapter Six

PIPING HOT MURDER

Wendy H. Jones

At the local Highland Games, high-end caterer Kirsty Callum's menu doesn't include murder. The local laird - and her former mentor - is found dead with hot treacle in his throat and her piping bag at the scene. The local police think it's accidental, but Kirsty is not so sure. Kirsty sets out to catch the killer hiding behind tartan, tartlets, and old grudges. Will she succeed or will the games be ruined.

When you consider pipes, drums and all things Scottish, death doesn't usually come skirling in to your mind performing a highland fling with merry abandon. Highland Games, the length and breadth of Scotland, are places of laughter, dancing, music and, of course, competition. From tossing of cabers and flinging of hammers to piping and strathspey reels, the world is out in force cheering on their favourite competitors and groaning when it doesn't go as planned. Tripping over a dead laird kills the mood instantly.

&

Death was far from the thoughts of Kirsty Callum when she looked out the window that morning to a sky so blue it could be the Caribbean. The loch, shrugging off its usual steely grey, had donned its best outlook and sparkled with iridescent light. For once, months of planning would not be ruined by rain. Monsoon level rain. The type seen in a typical Scottish summer. Instead of basking in this fortuitous turn of fate, the thought of all she had to do catapulted her from supine to vertical, and she hurried towards the bathroom. Taking her high-end, mobile restaurant, The Stag's Fork, to the games was a whole new level of responsibility. She was to be running the VIP restaurant in a huge marquee. She'd had the menu – Scottish fusion cuisine – planned for months and outlined the day to her staff in minute detail. But, with temperamental chefs (when weren't they) and waitresses who thought a broken fingernail was the ultimate disaster, she had to be on top of everything from the word go. Go meant now – silly o'clock on a glorious Saturday morning. Luckily, most of the prep had been done the day before, and the catering van – all 26 feet of top of the range, gleaming units and equipment - was already in place. By the time she got there, her sous chef should have her commis chefs beavering away preparing for the day ahead. Her events manager should be fussing over every minute detail of an already immaculately decorated marquee, now doubling as a restaurant. They were also setting up ready to host the prestigious Golden Sgian Dubh Awards, Scotland's most prestigious cooking competition. What could possibly go wrong when every step – from unpacking the marquees to packing them up again at late o'clock – had been meticulously planned right down to the last nano-second. Never mind a minute-by-minute planner, she had a second-by-second planner, and her staff would not dare to step to the left or right of it.

&

The activity on her arrival gave new meaning to the word bustling and set it on track to be hailed as frenzied. Whilst shoulders straightened when she appeared, no one stopped what they were doing or said anything more than a passing, 'Hello, Chef.' Not only was the sun in the heavens but all was well in her catering world.

Donning an apron, she immediately set to preparing her signature scorched treacle tartlets before popping them into the pre-heated oven. A feverish twenty minutes later a timer went off, and she checked the oven. Perfect. She lifted the tartlets from the oven and prepared to let them cool. The heavenly scent of fresh baking filled the air, making her drool. The smell was as nectar from the gods and informed her she'd got it bang on. She wiped her hands on a cloth.

'Fancy tart for a tart.'

Everyone in earshot kept shtum, but if dirty looks were anything to go by, they were horrified bordering on murderous.

The speaker, Alasdair Drummond, was her previous mentor but, by a weird twist of fate involving several mysterious accidents, he was now the local laird. The mentor/mentee relationship did not end well, so her gob was well and truly smacked when she was asked to do the VIP catering for this event. She suspected it had more to do with the estate management than the laird himself. She had a sudden urge to kick Drummond right in the canapes but shoved the thought deep inside for the sake of her fledgling business. Crippling your most prestigious customer was not a sensible career move; whatever the provocation. She was, however, about to throw him from her kitchen – that was her fiefdom, not his – when, with a final sneer, he disappeared in search of more pressing matters. If memory served her, these would probably involve a bottle of whisky.

'Are you okay?' Jamie, her sous chef, stood beside her, frowning.

'Peachy.' Kirsty tried for bravado, which made her feel better. She stuck out her chest. 'Nothing is going to ruin today.'

Jamie smiled. 'That's the ticket.' She hurried back to her cooking station.

Kirsty turned back to the tartlets, wondering if she should whip up an extra batch. She had enough pastry to do another fifty, but was that going overboard? She clingfilmed the dough and popped it aside; she could decide later. Too many tarts might not spoil the broth, but they would take up too much room. The motto in a mobile kitchen is - enough is enough - because there's no space for more.

She took a step backwards and crashed into someone. Swivelling, she faced the scowling face of Hamish Duffy.

'Stupid bitch. Can't you mind where you're going?'

Rapidly reevaluating her decision to temporarily hire her old rival, she snapped, 'Watch your tone.' Then, remembering the reason he needed the gig – his Michelin Star restaurant failed following a vile and scandalous review from Alasdair Drummond; something to do with rats and cockroaches if memory served – she softened her voice. 'We all need to get on if we're to pull this off. I know nerves are frazzled, but this is neither the time nor the place.'

His scowl faded, although it was still a mile short of a smile. 'Aye.' From Hamish, that was as good as an apology. He took the word taciturn to a whole new level of tac and turn. Never famed for being voluble, the ruining of both his restaurant and reputation turned his meagre talkative tap right off.

A soupcon of doubt crept into her thoughts – what if this all went a bit Pete Tong? Her bravado waved cheerily to her as it dashed out the door, making her stomach churn as fear wrapped its icy fingers around her midriff. With an event this big, failure was not an option or hers would be the next business going out of business. She mentally shrugged and pulled on her big chef's pants. This was not the time to be doubting herself. *You were born for such a time as this, Kirsty my girl.* She reached for her copy of the minute-by-minute, took a deep breath and straightened her apron.

The clock whizzed round as she darted from kitchen to marquee and back again. The marquee looked stunning, with tables and chairs bedecked with ribbons in ancient Maclaren Tartan. Candelabras were ready for lighting, silver cutlery gleamed even in the shade, and each place held a crisply starched napkin and a tartan favour bag filled with freshly baked shortbread. No expense was being spared - it was the event of the year.

Deciding it might be worth making another batch of burnt treacle tartlets – the likelihood was they would ask for more – she rolled out the pastry, popped it into the tins and pulled out the ingredients for the filling. Within minutes they were in a saucepan, and she was stirring like a whirling dervish. It was almost done when she heard a crash from the general direction of the marquee. She turned off the gas under the saucepan – adding a fire into the mix was not going to help the day go well - and leapt out the door.

As she feared, one of the temporary wait staff had tripped over a blade of grass and was lying on the ground groaning amidst a tsunami of broken teacups. Thankful she had hired way too many cups, and realising the young girl could not have been carrying more than a few, she bent towards her. 'Are you okay?'

The first aiders appeared, as if by magic, and declared

nothing more than her pride was hurt. The girl, Morag, said, 'Sorry, Miss.'

Kirsty reassured her that all was good and headed back towards the treacle tarts. She grabbed the spoon to give it a good mix, and then her eyebrows drew together. 'Who's used my filling?'

There were several cries of, 'Not me, Chef.'

Her voice rose. 'This is not funny. Not ever, but certainly not today.'

Everyone looked as innocent as a newborn. So, she quickly made up as many tartlets as she could.

She glanced at her Apple Watch, a present from her grandfather to say congratulations on the new business, pulled off her apron and dashed towards the catering tent. She needed an update from Morven Shaw, her events manager. Although efficient, she did seem a tad on the anxious side. Kirsty wasn't quite sure why, as she must be used to high powered events; according to her CV, she'd been the manager for several of them. That anxiety had Kirsty on edge and on top of every aspect of the day. In fact, she was rapidly wondering why she'd employed an events manager at all.

'How's it shaping up?'

Morven chewed on her lip. 'All going to schedule. But the laird's gone missing. He's meant to give the final sign off on everything I'm doing.'

Kirsty wasn't sure why Alisdair was all over her business like single cream. Then, she remembered the whole shebang was his personal fiefdom, and he was entitled to be all over any aspect of it.

'Has anyone gone to look for him?'

'They put something out over the Tannoy, and someone's been up to the castle.' More lip chewing. 'Still no sign.'

Kirsty took a deep breath and let it out slowly. Despite a secret feeling his absence was no loss, she realised it would be somewhat impossible to move forward without him. She took one step forward in sight of him; then, like the first act of a Victorian melodrama, a scream rent the air.

The room froze. 'What the...' She bolted towards the sound, followed by several of the staff. The remainder looked on with dropped jaws. Then murmurs started, quiet at first before reaching a crescendo worthy of the most energetic opera.

Kirsty screeched to a halt and did a spot of jaw dropping of her own. At the furthest reaches of the huge marquee, behind a display of brand-new, shiny dessert trolleys, lay the prostrate body of the laird. A young waitress stood next to him sobbing enough tears to float a super yacht. The mystery of the missing treacle filling was solved. It was currently stuffed into Alisdair Drummond's wide-open mouth. More than one man could ever eat. He was either extremely fond of treacle tart, or her filling had been used as a murder weapon. Fearing the latter, she dropped into the nearest chair. No stranger to death – she'd been brought up on a farm and animals died – murder was way out of her bailiwick. She was willing to lay bets murder by scorched treacle mix was one of the most unusual murder weapons.

Realising, as the main caterer and sole business represented, she was responsible for whatever happened next, she leapt from the seat and took charge.

She observed the assembled company. 'Don't just stand there, back to work.' Her tone brooked no argument. She grabbed Morven who was about to slink off. 'Not you.'

Morven's gazed at her, eyes wide.

'I know you're in shock but it's down to you and me. Phone the police.' Then she added for good measure, 'And an ambulance.'

'Can I do it further back.' Morgan trembled from head to toe.

'Yes. Then back to work. This show must go on. I'm hoping they'll contain the crime scene to the back of the marquee and use the back door opening.' She wanted to keep her events manager nose to grindstone to stop her having a complete meltdown. She was beginning to regret her choice of extra staff, then reminded herself they were both local and available. Also, the marquee did look stunning, and Morven had everyone working with great efficiency.

࿔

Any thoughts of the crime scene being contained flew out of the window with the arrival of the police. PC Fergus Ferguson seemed to be in charge. Everyone knew he was a truncheon short of a policeman. Why he'd been given his current position was another mystery no one could solve. and probably never would. Probably because nothing more than salmon poaching happened in this quiet neck of the woods. And even that was the odd salmon to feed the poacher's family, not mass theft. He probably spent more time making tea than he spent policing. Plus, he was probably the grandson or son-in-law of someone high up in Police Scotland.

This did not stop him using the full force of the law to start what was likely to be a shambolic investigation. 'Everyone out the way. Back. Back.' This was a trifle redundant given the only people there were the police. Also, he seemed to be letting his only two witnesses go. He really was as thick as a mealie pudding.

Kirsty obliged and pulled the young woman with her. She put an arm around her shoulders and said, 'What's your name?'

'Aisha.' The girl seemed to have perked up now that she was nowhere near the deceased and some of the shock had worn off. 'First time I've seen a dead body.' She shuddered. 'He looked affie. Like, all white.' Despite her name and Asian features, she very definitely hailed from Scotland if her accent was anything to go by.

'How did you find him, Aisha?'

'Like that. I never touched him. Honest.'

'I believe you.' She'd need to phrase her questions carefully.

They seemed to be divided by a common language. She sighed, feeling old.

'What were you doing when you found him?'

The young girl's eyes shifted somewhere left of Kirsty's face. 'Looking for something.' She tugged on her blouse which, given it was immaculate, needed no tugging or straightening.

'Something or someone?' She took in Aisha's trembling lip. 'You're not in trouble, but you need to be honest. The police will be asking you the same questions.'

'I was going to meet my boyfriend for five minutes.' Tears formed in her eyes. 'Please don't sack me. We need the money 'cause my dad's been made redundant.'

'No one is getting sacked. But when the police let you back to work, you need to be working, not sneaking around looking for your boyfriend.' Her voice held a hint of weariness. 'Did you see anyone else around?'

'No. Just the laird.' She thought for a moment and then added. 'I think the tent flap might have moved.' She shook her head. 'Nah. I might be making that up.'

Kirsty was of the opinion the wind probably moved the flap, although, thinking about it, there wasn't the merest hint of breeze today. Could the murderer have been slipping out the back? She shuddered at the thought; a few minutes earlier and the lass's dead body might have also been decorating the imitation parquet flooring. One corpse was enough for any VIP gathering.

PC Ferguson, known locally as Bumbling Bill, came storming up to them. 'What are you pair still doing here?'

'Waiting for you to interview us.' Kirsty's tone stayed low otherwise the useless idiot would slap her in handcuffs and arrest her before she could say false arrest.

'Yes. Well. I'd have found you.'

If they weren't law-abiding citizens, he'd be finding them on the road to Edinburgh by now. Then he'd pin the blame on someone else. Kirsty's main goal was to keep him from arresting them. She'd nothing to do with it, and by the looks of Aisha she didn't have the brains to work out a criminal master plan. The extent of her criminal activity would be smacking someone around the head with the mobile phone she was now using to doomscroll. Kirsty only hoped that nothing she was posting involved the corpse she'd discovered. She wasn't holding out much hope as the mantra seemed to be, if it's not on social media it didn't happen. Snapchat was probably breaking the internet with this news.

Still old school, Ferguson pulled out his notebook and a pencil.

I'm no lawyer, but surely a pencil wouldn't hold up in court. If it made it that far without being rubbed out or fading.

His next sentence had her wondering what the notebook was about. He'd obviously seen them do it on a cop show, which was where he got most of his information on policing from. How he'd managed to pass out of police college was a bigger mystery than that of the corpse.

'There's no need for witnesses.'

'You, what?' Kirsty was no police officer, but even she knew this was a bit strange.

He whipped out a bottle of Spiced Treacle Liqueur. Bare hands. No evidence bag. 'We found this. He obviously got drunk, then choked stuffing himself with treacle filling.' He threw her a look as if she were the one who was addled. 'You know what these toffs are like. Gluttons to a man.'

Kirsty had no words. She shook her head. Should she let someone higher up know about this? Yet, the doctor had put cause of death as choking, and the ambulancemen had carted him off to an undertaker, she presumed, so who was she to argue? Although the edges of her brain were whispering, *might not have been an accidental choking.*

'I need your names.'

That was something. Having both given their names, they were dismissed. Aisha scuttled off back to her duties, but Kirsty only wandered so far before turning back. 'Can we carry on with the games?'

"Of course.' Why would you cancel the games?'

Because the laird has shuffled off this mortal coil, and I'm still convinced he was helped in his shuffling. Still, if they were convinced it was natural causes it meant she could carry on with the dinner. Yes, she was sad he'd met his demise, but the show must go on. He certainly wouldn't have cared if the shoe had been on the other foot. He'd have blamed her for the inconvenience and carried on without another thought, promoting one of the other chefs and bullying them into doing his bidding.

She checked everyone was doing their job and everything was proceeding at a satisfactory pace despite the setback, before hurrying back to the kitchen. She broke the news Fergus was dead. They looked genuinely shocked, although she could swear Hamish's face broke out in a smile. She wasn't surprised, given the history between him and their corpse. Time was marching on, so she took a look at her venison cherry canapes. Perhaps a smidgeon more cherry sauce was needed. She rummaged through the piping bags and chose one. It was a tad too big, but someone had obviously got there before her. In a catering trailer, it was first-come, first-served. Finesse meant the bag size wasn't that important, and the extra cherry sauce was just what was needed to lift the canapes out of the ordinary and into the extraordinary. Her stomach rumbled. Maybe she should try a couple to make sure they were perfect. And a couple of the other canapés. There were more than enough, and she hadn't eaten anything other than half a slice of toast all day. She shoved them in her mouth whole, and barely chewed before she swallowed. Come to think of it, she'd not had anything to drink. She grabbed a coffee and sat on the steps of the trailer. Inhaling the heady aroma of the fresh brew, she made a valiant attempt to clear her mind for five minutes but thoughts of Alasdair Drummond's body lying on the imitation parquet tap-danced in her brain. *How could anyone choke to death on pudding? Even if they were drunk. If he was that drunk, how in the heck did he steal my pie filling without anyone noticing? Why did he bother going all the way to the back of the marquee to eat it? The maths ain't mathing. Something was rotten in this wee village, and she could almost smell it.*

She jumped up and went to check on how things were proceeding for the dinner.

'All proceeding to plan, Chef.' Jamie didn't stop working. She was shaping up to be a real asset.

'You can call me Kirsty. I've told you often enough.'

'Wouldn't be right in here.'

Wherever she trained, they certainly did it right. 'I'll be back in about ten minutes. You're in charge.'

Jamie looked up, eyes wide. 'Me?'

'Yes, you. It's only ten minutes, not the entire banquet.' She smiled. 'You've got this.'

The young chef's smile could have warmed up leftovers. She turned back to the task at hand.

For good measure, Kirsty wandered around to check the others. All hard at it, and all looked like they knew what they were doing. The young man doing the dishes was scrubbing hard enough to wash away all the sins of the world. She knew he wanted to be a chef someday, and this was his foot in the door. Resting a hand on his skinny shoulder, she said, 'You're doing a great job.'

'Thank you, Chef. I won't let you down, Chef.'

'I know you won't.'

She turned on her heel and headed towards her sleuthing, a determined bounce in her step and an even more determined glint in her eye.

Entering the marquee, the major flaw in her plan quickly occurred to her. Everyone who was currently bustling around had been bustling like demons whilst the murder took place.

Well, not quite everyone, as the only bustle the murderer was doing was helping the Laird to meet his maker. How on earth was she going to interview all these people? This was taking impossible to a whole new level. Deciding to park interviewing for the time being, she headed towards the former crime scene. A brief but thorough search was called for.

Given she was wearing chef's whites, it was also a rather tentative search. Getting her whites stained with food was one thing crawling around on the floor was another. She did her best with the various nooks and crannies and was rewarded. 'Eureka.' She hauled out her missing piping bag from between two stacks of spare chairs. One sniff told her it reeked of treacle tart filling. Thankful she'd shoved on some gloves before she left the catering trailer, she held it tightly until she could pop it in a clean bag. She knew PC Plod, the stupid sod, a.k.a. PC Ferguson, had made a right hash of this investigation. She'd say made a right hash of the search, but she wasn't convinced he'd done one. She looked around some more and found an iPhone under one of the chairs. Probably belonged to one of the teens who'd sneaked back here to look at it, although she wasn't sure they'd stay away.

She headed to the storage area of the marquee and grabbed a couple of the brown paper bags which were to be used later for those taking food home. Then, she phoned her bestie. It was time for reinforcement.

Mere minutes later, Leanne Morrison flew through the door like the entire massed bands were chasing her. 'Trainee investigator reporting for duty.' She snapped a smart salute, a hangover from her Royal Air Force days.

'I'm not exactly an expert myself but I'm sure something smells fishy, and I'm not talking about the Bradon Rost Smoked Salmon with Whisky.'

'So, what are my duties?'

'Interrogation of as many of the staff milling around in the marquee.' She took in the look on her friend's face and added an extra frisson of complexity. 'You've only got about twenty minutes to do it in.'

'Eh?... What?...' The are you mad look turned to one of sheer panic.

'Off you go. Gossip like you've never gossiped before. I've a kitchen to run.' She waved her hands in a shooing motion. 'I'll make sure I'm free in about twenty-five minutes.'

Leanne, easy-going and used to her friend's ways, trotted off as though she were doing her RAF fitness test.

Kirsty turned towards the kitchen. The delicious aroma of meat, fish and game assaulted her nostrils as she entered the kitchen. That smell told her every dish would be cooked to perfection and ready just at the right time to ensure triumph when served to their elite guests. How those elite guests would feel about the guest of honour being AWOL was another matter altogether. Way above her pay grade. She titivated and tarted, watched and instructed, praised and chivvied until rapping on the door signified Leanne's entry.

Kirsty grabbed two glasses of water and pulled her friend outside and behind the trailer.

'Whoa. Whoa. Not so fast.' Leanne yanked her arm away.

'I've no time for finesse unless I'm finessing food. What's the gossip?'

'I've a mind not to tell you.' Her smile and the amused glint in her eyes indicated she was about to spill all. They also indicated all might just be juicy.

'As suspected, everybody knows everyone and everything around here. They were keener than keen to spill the beans.'

'Fab. Spit it out then.'

'I'll stick to what might be salient. I'm sure you're not interested in who's going out with whom when it comes to the youngsters' love lives.'

'Yep. Short and snappy.'

'Morven Shaw is a spurned ex-girlfriend. Actually, more than that, they were partners.'

'Nothing new there. They parted on good terms.'

'Oh no they didn't. It would appear our Alasdair had some dirt on her and was about to dish it in the way of an exposé.'

'Sorry?'

'Would have been the end of Morven's career.' She paused for a few seconds to take in Kirsty's face, ad added, 'Then there is Tosin Akinwande.'

'Who's he?'

'Our freshly dead laird was mentoring him until yesterday. Then...' She paused for dramatic effect. 'Alisdair decided to publicly lambast him and fired him in front of an audience.'

'What's that got to do with us or the death today?'

'Tosin is currently keeping body and soul together by working as a waiter for our dinner.'

It wasn't often Kirsty was taken aback but her aback was currently well and truly taken. 'So, two people with the means and the motive.' She thought for a minute. 'And they were in the vicinity.'

'Oh, it doesn't end there.' She shook her head. 'One of your chefs, Hamish Duffy, has been spreading it around that he was going to get Alasdair for ruining him.'

'Grief. I know catering can be a hotbed of intrigue but never so hot it could lead to murder.'

'Makes me glad I'm an accountant.'

Kirsty looked at her friend, askance. She was more than an accountant. She was actually CEO of one of the biggest financial firms in Scotland. 'Three key players.' Time was of the essence as she needed this sorted before the dinner started. Then she remembered the iPhone. Alasdair was taking photos in her kitchen with one. She wondered if it held any clues as to the killer.

'Hang fire.' She dashed off and returned with the phone. 'Can you get into this?'

Leanne had done a course on forensic accounting, and cracking into phones, tablets and computers was part of it. She grabbed the phone and touched the screen. 'It doesn't take much getting into. It's not password protected at all.'

'Can you tell who it belongs to?'

A few more taps. 'Our corpse. We shouldn't be doing anything with this. It's evidence.'

'What evidence? Fergus declared it an accident. No crime. No evidence.'

Leanne shrugged, although her face said she wasn't convinced.

'Can you get into anything?'

A few more taps and swipes. 'Everything.'

Kirsty looked at her watch. 'Quick. Anything incriminating?'

More taps. Leanne squinted at the screen and then her eyes grew wide.

'What? What's going on?'

Leanne handed the phone over. 'Here. Read it yourself.'

After a couple of minutes of reading she reeled back, her face frozen. When she could speak, she said, 'The whole sordid truth written in minute detail.' The exposé was of cheating in the games event world, which could ruin Morven. In a sordid twist, it would appear that Hamish was also up to his well-muscled neck in nefarious deeds.

'Can you ask Morven and Tosin to come over here in about five minutes. Tell them it's for a final briefing and I need Tosin to do something for me.'

Leanne did as requested.

Kirsty made a quick phone call then headed inside the van. She made sure everything was going well. 'You're doing a top job, Jamie. There will be a sizeable bonus in your paycheque.'

Jamie's cheeks flared bright red. 'Thank you, Chef. I'm doing my best.'

Morven and Tosin appeared, and Kirsty called over to Hamish, 'Can you join us for a minute?'

They huddled just inside the door of the pantry, Kirsty clutching something in a brown paper bag.

'I'm going to get to the point. 'I think one, or even a couple of you, murdered Alasdair Drummond.'

'Rubbish. The police declared he choked when he was drunk.' Belligerence beamed out from every one of Hamish's suddenly sweaty pores.

'This pair,' Morven pointed to the others, might have had motive, 'but he and I were the best of pals.'

'I beg to differ; he was about to spill the beans on a scandal involving you.'

The colour drained from her face. 'That was utter lies, but I still didn't kill him.'

Kirsty pulled out the piping bag. 'I believe you. Squeezing this while holding a man would be difficult for someone as slight as you. Also, how would you get my filling?'

She turned to Tosin. 'You're off the hook too. You might have hated him but getting the murder weapon from my kitchen would be nigh on impossible.

She turned to the now copiously sweating Hamish. 'That leaves you. Not only did he ruin your reputation once, he was about to do it again. You're strong as an ox, have the motive and the means.'

'I've been here the whole time.'

'No, you've not. Jamie confirmed you disappeared at about the right time. Apparently, you were going to the toilet. Yeah, right. You went to rendezvous with our victim.'

Hamish, defeated, thought it was time to fess up. 'Okay. I did. But I only wanted to scare him. He was drunker than drunk on the bottle of Spiced Treacle liqueur I gave him. I knew he'd down it immediately, the old soak. I wanted to give him a scare, but got carried away and shoved too much scalding pie filling in. I panicked when he choked.' Then, he pulled himself to his full height, shoved Kirsty aside and ran out the door.

Straight into the waiting arms of Kirsty's boyfriend, who happened to be a police sergeant from the nearby town. He'd been enjoying the games with his mother and two boys when he got the call from Kirsty. He slapped some handcuffs on their suspect, leaving Kirsty wondering why he was wandering around with handcuffs in his pocket. He hauled him off to wait for the backup he'd called for.

☙

The dinner was a triumph, with the crowning glory being the Scorched Treacle Tartlets with Whisky Cream. As Kirsty suspected, there were calls for more and every last crumb was mopped up and eaten. Following the awards, one of the national cooking magazines interviewed Kirsty and told her there would be a full four-page spread in the next issue. She was also asked to cater the games again the following year.

Yes, the murder may have been piping hot, but not too hot for her to handle.

BIO:

Wendy H. Jones is a multi-award-winning, best-selling Scottish author of crime thrillers, cozy mysteries, children's picture books and non-fiction books for authors. She won the Books Go Social Book of the Year at Dublin writers conference and the prestigious Scottish Association of Writers, Janetta Bowie Chalice for best non-fiction book She is also an acclaimed international public speaker teaching writing craft and marketing, worldwide. In addition, she is the Editor in Chief of Writers' Narrative eMagazine, a partner in Auscot Publishing and Retreats and owner of Scott and Lawson Publishing.

RECIPE

Treacle Tartlets
Best served without a side dish of murder

Ready rolled shortcut (or gluten free) pastry – yes I know we should be making it from scratch, but I'm of the mind life is too short to be making it from scratch. Especially when there is crime to be solved.
Please can the purists amongst us forgive me

Filling
350 g (12 oz) Lyle's golden syrup
25 g (1 oz) butter or margarine
finely grated rind and juice of 1 lemon
75 g (3 oz) fresh white breadcrumbs (regular or gluten free)
beaten egg or milk for glazing

Roll out the pastry and use to line the cake tin.
To make the filling, warm the golden syrup in a heavy-based pan with the butter and lemon rind and juice.
Sprinkle the breadcrumbs evenly over the base of the pastry case, then slowly pour in the melted syrup.
Make strips from the remainder of the pastry and place these over the tart in a lattice pattern, brushing the ends with water to stick them to the pastry.
Brush with a small amount of beaten egg or milk.
Bake in the oven at 190°C (375°F) 25--30 minutes until the filling is firm.

Serve with a scoop of whisky ice cream and a wee dram of whisky cream liqueur.

Chapter Seven

MURDER AT MI CORAZÓN: A KITCHEN WITH SECRETS

Nicolette Lemmon

It's a busy night for Chef Clau Rios and her right-hand woman, Jen Watson, who recently opened their dream Mexican vegan restaurant, Mi Corazon, in Houston, Texas. When a scream from the dining room dashes hopes for a good review when the lifeless body of the food critic slumped over his Killer Street Tacos. Chef Claus is a suspect so Jen must find the culprit to save her friend and the restaurant.

The Taste of Power

Mi Corazón, the new vegan restaurant on the Kemah Boardwalk, pulsed with life on the night of Paul Henderson's final meal.

Laughter traveled on the cool air from the bay and the heart-shaped neon sign glowed brightly, enticing patrons in for dinner. From the moment the doors opened, tension simmered under the aroma of cumin, blistered chilies, and wood-fired tortillas. Waiters glided around tables like dancers, while the kitchen behind glowed with heat, sweat, and adrenaline.

At the heart of it all stood Chef Claudia Rios - known to staff and patrons as Chef Clau. A knife in one hand, a tasting spoon in the other, her white coat was already damp with effort, her long dark locks tied back with a bandana. Driving the restaurant business daily with Chef Clau was Jen Watson, the managing partner in Mi Corazón.

Tonight, the presence of Paul Henderson, a sharp-tongued media critic, had flipped the entire staff onto high alert. Clau had not seen Paul since his now-infamous review for the Mi Corazón grand opening, comparing Clau's version of Oaxacan Mole Negro to 'burnt pudding mixed with engine oil.' That review had cost Mi Corazón a successful start to their innovative vegan menu. It had forced Chef Clau and Jen into damage control to keep the restaurant open by cutting menu prices and trying to lure customers in with specials.

Now he was back. Sitting at table nine. Smiling.

'Don't worry,' murmured Carmen Garcia Rodriguez, Clau's sous chef. Her voice was low and steady, like always. 'You've got this with your new Killer Street Tacos.'

'Thanks for the confidence,' Clau muttered. 'You've known him a long time, right?'

Carmen nodded. 'Unfortunately, yes. He took down my family's restaurant with a critical review a few years ago.' She paused. 'Happy to have found a spot with you and Jen.'

Jen walked over and patted Carmen on the shoulder. Before

heading back to the office, Jen added, 'Well, he's already eaten the Citrus Cauliflower Ceviche. Hey, he didn't spit it out, so that's progress.'

Clau laughed. Jen's calm helped. Tonight, with the entire future of their restaurant under a microscope, they both needed to be rock steady.

Turning to Diego Serrano, the front-of-house server for table nine, Carmen handed him a plated dip and warm corn tortilla chips. 'Keeping my fingers crossed he likes this Mango Munch Salsa.' With a smirk, Carmen added, 'Don't forget to tell him our chips are handmade here in the kitchen, we don't need to give him any reasons to try to bring us down next.'

The Critic's Shadow

Across the room, Paul Henderson dined alone as his eyes scanned every dish with an element of suspicion. Occasionally, he scribbled notes in a small journal.

He didn't speak to staff – maintaining a haughty air. When Diego laid down the appetizer, he quietly announced, 'This is our Mango Munch Salsa with Black Bean & Tajin and our home-made chips.'

Diego then placed a folded note next to the appetizer plate.

'What's this?' Paul asked, reaching for the note.

'I was asked to leave it but didn't read it,' Diego swore. 'I just put it in my pocket.'

The critic unfolded the note, read it and angrily crumpled and tossed it on the floor.

In the kitchen, the main course being plated for the critic was a new recipe that Chef Clau developed for Seitan Fajita Tacos. Because the protein ingredient, seitan, sounded similar to 'Satan,' Jen suggested naming the dish, 'Killer Street Tacos.' With avocado, strips of spiced seitan, seasonings and garnishes, the dish had become an instant showstopper.

A couple minutes later, Miguel Martinez, the young dishwasher and busser, followed Diego out to clear the critic's appetizer plate. As Miguel slipped back into the kitchen, Diego presented the main course with a flourish. As he leaned down to tell Paul the name of the dish, someone brushed past table nine, bumping against him causing a stumble toward Paul. The critic looked up with an angry expression.

'Excuse me, sir,' Diego hurriedly apologized and went to check on another table.

A minute later, Paul leaned forward, studying the plate. He lifted his fork - then froze.

A cough. Sharp. Then another.

Paul dropped his utensil and reached for his throat, eyes widening. He slumped forward without a sound, collapsing onto the plate with terrifying stillness.

Time fractured. A scream from a nearby table. Silverware clattered.

Diego turned in surprise and shouted for help.

❧

The Nightmare Begins

The loud cry from the dining room alerted Clau and Jen. They rushed to the kitchen door, swinging it wide and found themselves faced with chaos. Customers were jumping up from their tables, pointing to a man who lay slumped over his plate.

Clau gasped. 'Oh my God...who—'

'Geez, it's him,' cried Carmen as she walked towards them from the dining room.

Jen pulled her phone out and dialed 9-1-1 as she followed Clau, making her way through the doorway to get a better look. Clau's voice shook as she whispered, 'Yes, it's Paul Henderson. The food critic.'

Jen's face twisted into horror. 'The ambulance is on its way.'

The restaurant staff gathered behind Jen and Clau at the kitchen door, murmuring in shock. Tonight, everyone on staff was hoping he would love the new recipes Chef Clau had developed to impress him. That hope flew out the window with the commotion in the dining room and a wailing ambulance siren.

Whispers began about an allergy or heart attack.

'Let's help calm the situation. Diego, get takeout boxes to allow the customers to leave. I'm not worried about their bills. Then, Miguel, start getting the kitchen cleared,' ordered Jen.

Detective Alvarez Arrives

Outside the restaurant, Detective Mark Alvarez stepped under the glow of the Mi Corazón neon heart sign, smoothing down his slick black hair, and surveying the chaos inside.

He had grown up in Seabrook, just a few miles from Kemah Boardwalk. He marveled at the metamorphosis of the area from the early 90s into a fun dining and entertainment venue. While used to eating daily at tamale carts and food trucks, Alvarez felt funny walking into a fancy place with $18 cocktails.

As he strolled into the crazy scene, the detective noted the paramedics had lain the critic on the restaurant floor and were working to revive him. It seemed like this was just an unfortunate medical emergency, Alvarez was unsure why he had been called to the scene so, he began to scan the area for evidence.

No signs of trauma. No weapon. No blood.

In fact, at first glance it would seem like an unfortunate event and not a police matter.

Searching for the owners, Alvarez noted that guests were ushered out with their 'to go' boxes while Jen and Clau stood like statues by the kitchen door.

Flashing his badge at the two women, he pulled a small notebook out of his jacket. 'Detective Alvarez, Kemah Police Department, and you are?' He waited patiently for the two women to answer.

'I'm Jen and this is Chef Clau. We're the owners.'

Jotting down their answers, Alvarez nodded toward the paramedics. 'The name of the customer?'

'Paul Henderson,' Jen side-eyed Clau. 'Our server, Diego, alerted us to his collapse.'

With a nod, Clau asked, 'Why were you called? It surely is an allergic reaction or—'

Alvarez stopped her by raising his hand. 'True, but we're called if there is no immediate way to determine the cause or it presents a threat to public safety. I will need to interview the server, Diego.'

Jen left to get Diego while Alvarez turned to Chef Clau. 'And what did he eat and drink before the incident?'

After Chef Clau recited the menu items, Alvarez thanked her and moved away to talk to Diego.

The dining room was quiet as all the customers had left. The paramedics rolled the gurney with the unconscious critic hooked up to fluids out to the waiting ambulance in the parking lot.

Chef Clau's shoulders slumped as she walked back through the kitchen toward the office. Before entering she tossed off her gloves, hugged herself, and squeezed her soft brown eyes tightly shut.

'How horrible. Maybe I'm not meant to have my own place,' she whispered. The dream was to make her mark in vegan Mexican cuisine in a fun partnership with Jen. Instead, the dining room was cluttered with medical supplies and half-finished meals. 'Hope nothing else goes wrong.'

As she sulked into the office to sit down at her desk, something caught her eye. The safe door on the wall behind the desk was ajar, and empty. She ran out into the kitchen, calling for Jen.

'What is it?' Jen appeared with a concerned look.

'Money – our savings – gone,' stuttered Clau pointing to the safe.

Jen rushed over to the safe and found it empty of the thousands they had kept for emergencies.

'Crap, I was making the bank deposit when the loud commotion started and must have left the safe open,' Jen brushed a hand through her short blonde hair. Tears welled up in her eyes as she turned back to Clau. 'I am so sorry. But who would do this?'

Clau shrugged and looked around at the staff who had gathered in the kitchen.

One person was missing.

Miguel was nowhere to be seen.

Jen hurried into the dining room to find Alvarez. 'Can you please come to our office? We have a problem.'

Showing the safe to the detective, Jen added, 'It's crazy, it seems that during the emergency in the dining room, someone came in and helped themselves to about $20,000 from our safe.'

'Could it have been someone from your staff?'

Clau sighed. 'Yep. And Miguel, our dishwasher, is missing.'

Alvarez looked across the kitchen. 'Probably out the back door?'

Both women nodded. A tear escaped down Clau's cheek.

Moving to a file cabinet, Jen pulled out the personnel file on Miguel and handed it to the detective.

'Is there anyone else who had access and might have taken the money?' Alvarez looked over Diego's file.

Jen and Clau exchanged frightened looks. 'The staff know about the safe - but access? Not usually because only Jen and I have the combination.'

Alvarez looked back and forth at the two with a quizzical expression. He waited.

Jen cleared her throat and said, 'I was doing the bank deposit and had opened the safe but rushed to the dining room when everything happened.'

❧

Heart Broken

News had broken overnight from the local media about the death of Paul Henderson. Television crews were parked outside the boardwalk. In the morning, both Clau and Jen went in the back door to avoid the reporters and the crazy scene. Some cameramen were even standing directly outside the restaurant's front door.

Mi Corazón remained closed. 'My Heart' was broken and needed to heal.

The two women worked silently as they set about to clean up the dining room. After some time, Jen finally stopped and said, 'Geez, a negative review would have been better than this.'

The phone rang. Detective Alverez cut right to the point.

'Wanted to let you know that we are now looking at the death of Paul Henderson as an unexpected or suspicious death,' said Alverez. 'There was no clear indication of heart attack or allergy, so the body is at the coroner. I will need to come by and interview you and the employees that were there that night.'

Clau hung her head. It wasn't over. 'We're still closed, Detective, so only the two of us are here. It might take time to call the others in, or do you want their numbers?'

'Yes, I can call to set something up with each of your staff. I will need to come by to talk with both of you as well.'

'But you did ask us questions last night. Why would you need to talk with us?' Clau asked.

Jen cut in, 'Yes, and what about the stolen money? Any leads or have you found Miguel?'

Alvarez cleared his throat. 'First, the death occurred at this restaurant, but it's been cleaned. That means evidence has been compromised, so I am forced to find ways to uncover what happened. Starting with you two.' He paused. 'Second, the address on Miguel's application was a fake. We put out an APB to get officers looking for him.' Alvarez paused. 'Also, we did find he had a prior criminal record for petty theft as a teen. But it was suppressed as underage, so even if you would have run a background check, nothing would have appeared.'

Clau groaned.

Raising her hands in confusion, Jen demanded. 'So, where do we stand for reopening?'

Alvarez shook his head. 'Closed until we hear from the coroner, I'll let you know.'

Click. Silence.

🐌

The Coroner's Result

Two days later, Jen was setting up the dining room to be ready for when the all-clear comes from the detective. Her cell phone buzzed. It was Alvarez.

Finally. Fingers crossed for good news.

'Hello, Ms. Watson, we actually had to review this with the medical examiner,' Alvarez gave a pregnant pause.

Jen was anxious. 'And?

'The medical examiner has determined there was a neurotoxin, something plant-based, absorbed through skin contact or injection. There was a tiny pinprick on the side of Henderson's neck.' Alvarez offered a few more details of the crime as Jen listened with intent.

Barely visible. Almost missed. Fast acting.

'So, Paul Henderson was murdered?' Jen's big blue eyes bulged. She waved Clau from the dining room.

'Yes. I'm headed to the restaurant and will need to talk with you and Clau,' said Alvarez. The phone went silent.

'Clau, the detective has terrible news. Henderson was murdered,' Jen said, shock still resting on her face. 'And he's coming to talk with us.'

Clau stopped walking toward Jen and hung her head in despair. 'Could this get any worse?'

A banging fist at the front door announced Alvarez. Jen rushed to unlock it and let the detective into the quiet dining room.

He motioned to Clau to follow him as he walked into the Mi Corazón office. She sat with her arms crossed; jaw clenched.

'I saw the bad review he gave your Mole Negro,' began Alvarez. 'You know how bad this looks.'

Clau didn't flinch. 'It seemed he hated my recipe. Sure. But I didn't kill him. You said it was a prick of a poison, not my Killer Street Tacos, right?'

'True, but did you ever have words with Henderson?'

'Never saw him up close. That night, I watched him a few times at the pass-through.'

'And Jen?'

Clau hesitated. 'She's moving all the time, doing the hosting, checking on patrons, and coming in the kitchen to check on order flow. We both were furious with Paul for criticizing our food. It caused a huge downturn in our new business. But she would never do something like that.'

Alvarez had heard enough people say those words, only to eat them in court. 'Who reached out to him to come back that night?'

'I did.'

Jotting a note in his ever-present journal, Alvarez frowned. 'That'll be all. Ask Jen to come in to answer some questions.'

'Sure, but do you have an update on finding Miguel or our money?' Clau asked, eyebrows raised.

With a shake of his head, Alvarez said, 'No, but we learned that he lives with his mother and have contacted her.'

Clau said, 'Didn't think so.' And with a shrug, she huffed off to find Jen.

Motioning his hand to a chair, Jen sat across from the detective.

'With the death of the critic and the issue with the missing money, I failed to ask if you have any security cameras. They might have caught something on both crimes,' started Alvarez.

'We only had one at the back door, so we checked it that night. Unfortunately, it was off, not recording. It was unplugged. Odd because it's been on since we opened.'

'Were any of your employees familiar with the camera?' Alvarez poised his pen over the notebook.

'Maybe,' Jen rubbed her temples. 'If we make it through this, I'll need to ramp up our security.'

Making some notes, Alvarez looked straight at Jen. 'Give me an accounting of your movements from that night.'

After asking questions for almost 30 minutes, Alvarez flipped his notebook shut and put it back in his jacket pocket. 'That's it for now. While I did one-on-one interviews of your staff, with this new development, I need to circle back around. If we give the okay to reopen, can you call the staff in for a meeting so I can talk to them again?'

Jen nodded. 'Anything else, Detective?'

'One last question.' He paused. 'Because you already suspect Miguel took the money, any idea about who could have poisoned the critic?'

'Nope. The staff were all excited to give him a good experience to get a good review.' Jen paused. 'But now with the demise of the critic and no money, it's going to be hard to stay open for very long.'

🔥

Staff Interviews

Someone had killed a patron. With poison. In Mi Corazón.

As the staff sat waiting to be interviewed by Alvarez, the whispers began about who it could have been. To poison one of the patrons seemed unbelievable. Eyes shot to Diego. He was the one serving the critic. He had access by serving up the dishes.

Plus, money was missing. Quiet, curly-haired Miguel was gone. How could it be that a young busser with a sweet smile would steal from the restaurant?

A hush fell as the detective called Diego's name, who stood to go into the office, pale and shaking. Motioning to the chair in front of the desk, the detective flipped to a new journal page and looked hard at the server.

'Can you walk me through the evening from the moment you first encountered the victim?'

Diego began describing the evening. He recited the dishes brought to the critic and then paused. 'I was given a folded note to hand to Mr. Henderson.' He hurriedly added, 'But I didn't read it.'

Frowning, Alvarez asked, 'First, where is the note?'

'When Mr. Henderson had his episode, I went to the table to see what was wrong. It was on the floor, so I just picked it up. Reflex of clearing tables, I guess.' Diego pulled a paper out of his jeans pocket and handed it to the detective.

On the paper was a typed message, '*You have ruined your last family restaurant. You're done.*'

'Second, who gave you this note?' Diego's apprehension was obvious as he shifted back and forth. 'She gave it to me. I...I didn't think it mattered.'

'Who?' pressed Alvarez.

Diego looked down at his hands and quietly said, 'Carmen.'

'Thank you, Diego, can you send her in?'

While waiting for Carmen to come in, Alvarez fired off an email ordering a deeper background check on the sous chef.

Carmen's interview was strange. She was polite. Calm. Maybe too calm.

'Carmen, can you give me an accounting of what you saw that night, specifically any interactions with Paul Henderson?'

'I prepped food, I plated, I stayed out of sight.'

For several minutes, Carmen recounted being in the kitchen and plating the appetizers. She was adamant about not leaving the kitchen until she heard the shouts and commotion from the dining room.

Frowning as he looked down at his notebook, Alvarez asked, 'Here in my notes, Diego said you gave him a folded paper to give Henderson. Is that true?'

Still as a frightened rabbit, Carmen cleared her throat. 'That was something that -um-Miguel gave me to have Diego take to the critic.' She paused. 'Didn't look at it.'

Tapping his pen on the desk, Alvarez stared at the sous chef. 'So, once again, you didn't go into the dining room until after the commotion started?'

Carmen shook her head. 'No.' She paused. 'We're getting ready to reopen, so can I go now? Lots to do.'

'Fine. If I have more questions, I will find you.'

❧

Confrontation

The name 'Carmen Garcia Rodriguez' wasn't her real name. Alvarez flipped through the report to find she was really Carmelita Rivas Delgado, linked to the failed family restaurant in Seabrook called Estrella De Mar, 'Sea Star,' owned by her grandparents who then passed it to her parents. The restaurant had a successful run for almost fifty years until, according to a media story in the report, after a critic's scathing review, the restaurant was forced to close.

The critic? There it was – Paul Henderson.

Alvarez wasn't surprised that Carmen had created a pseudonym to hide the association with the failed restaurant. Now she was a simple sous chef, not the owner.

Even more poignant, Carmen now worked at a new restaurant that had faced the same critic's negativity.

The detective didn't wait. He left the precinct and returned to Mi Corazón that night as Clau and Jen were finishing the prep for reopening.

'Need to speak with Carmen. Is she here?' he asked them.

'Yes, she's prepping in the kitchen. Want to use our office? I can bring her in,' Jen offered.

Carmen didn't run. Didn't even blink. His eyes followed her as she sat in the same chair as the day before.

Alvarez dropped a folder on the desk, leaned back in his chair and sat with arms crossed. 'Let's start with why you altered your identity, Carmelita.'

'I don't know what you mean.' Carmen looked away.

The detective tapped the folder in front of him. 'It's right here in this background check.'

Eyes wide, Carmen stared at him. 'It's a pseudonym, no harm with that.'

'Unless you're trying to hide something. But let's switch gears,' stated Alvarez. 'You ever heard of curare?'

'No, why?'

'Seems that Henderson was poisoned by a neurotoxin, fairly certain it was curare, 'said Alvarez. 'It's known as the South American arrow poison. Where was your family originally from?'

Silence.

'Says here in the report that your grandparents emigrated from Ecuador.'

Carmen shifted in her chair. 'That doesn't mean anything.'

Pushing the note toward Carmen, he watched her expression. 'One thing you forgot was the note. You may have gotten rid of the poison, but there are fingerprints on the note. Yours and Diego's. But you said Miguel gave you the note, and his were not.' He sat forward with his elbows on the desk. 'And we checked with Miguel's mother, who said this was his first restaurant job. The person writing the note had a history with the critic's negative reviews.'

More silence.

'Your family lost their restaurant after he went on TV, destroying the reputation of the 50-year-old establishment, right?'

Carmen grimaced at the mention of the failed family business.

'Why,' Alvarez said softly. 'Revenge?'

Carmen's voice was low. 'You don't have anything to connect me with this conjecture.'

'Well, you claimed not to go out in the dining room, yet Diego thought it was you who bumped into him and then the critic,' Alvarez said. 'All it took was to lean in, one small prick behind the ear. So gentle he didn't even feel it.'

Carmen stared out the window.

'He was going to do it again. Destroy another restaurant?' Alvarez pushed.

'I didn't want to hurt Clau. Or the restaurant. I just needed to protect Mi Corazón from him.'

'Carmen Garcia Rodriguez also known as Carmelita Rivas Delgado, I am placing you under arrest for the murder of Paul Henderson.' Alvarez walked around the desk, had her stand up and cuffed her. 'You have the right to remain silent...'

§

Resolution of Secrets

The story exploded online: Famous Critic Killed by Chef's Right Hand. Some people say any publicity is good publicity for a business. But even with the murder solved, the theft still hung over Clau and Jen.

Where was their money? Would they ever see their twenty grand again?

In the throes of the hiring process for a dishwasher and sous chef, Detective Alvarez walked into the restaurant and interrupted Clau and Jen with good news. Miguel's mom convinced her son to finally come forward. He explained to the women how Miguel had stashed most of the money in a mattress at his mom's house.

'So, ladies, it looks like you'll get most of your money back.'

The women hugged the stoic detective in celebration that at least all was not lost.

Alvarez stood in the kitchen as Clau returned to the chef's counter, slicing limes with mechanical precision.

'She didn't do it for us,' Clau said without looking up. 'She did it for her family's ruined legacy.'

'True, yet now her legacy is murder and prison time,' offered Alvarez.

Jen came to stand next to the detective. 'It's shocking to have not one but two employees that committed crimes.'

'You hadn't vetted either one, so you couldn't have known, right?'

Clau's eyes flicked up, burning. 'I trusted Carmen's – er – Carmelita's cooking skills.'

'And I trusted young, charming Miguel,' added Jen. 'Since he came clean, I hope they go easy on him when he goes to court.'

The women asked Alverez to stay and soon a happier Chef Clau placed a warm plate of Killer Street Tacos in front of him.

Sometimes justice didn't taste like victory. Sometimes it just tasted like lime, smoke, and fresh avocado.

Alvarez smiled and ate silently. 'At least Mi Corazón no longer has a broken heart.'

BIO:

Nicolette Lemmon, the innovative founder of LemmonTree Marketing Group, has authored several non-fiction books including *Write. Market. Succeed. An Author's Marketing Playbook*. As a mystery writer, she's a member of Sisters in Crime, an international crime writers organization, serving on the Marketing and Education committees. Nicolette is a founding member and past president of the Sisters in Crime Grand Canyon Writers chapter. In addition, after a career of providing cutting-edge marketing seminars, webinars and conferences, Nicolette has focused on bringing her expertise to writing groups across the country in various genres. She lives in Scottsdale, Arizona, USA.

RECIPE

Seitan Fajita Tacos

Fajita Ingredients
1 onion
1tbsp avocado oil
4 medium seitan steaks
2 bell peppers
Salt and pepper to taste
Tortillas

Guacamole Ingredients
½ onion
1 tomato
½ C cilantro
1 serrano pepper (optional)
1 large avocado
Juice of 1 lime
Salt and pepper to taste

Tortilla Ingredients
2 cups masa harina
1¼ cups water

Method
Slice the onion and cook it in a skillet with the avocado oil until softened. Cut the seitan steaks into thin strips and add them to the skillet. Cook until golden brown. Slice the bell peppers into strips, add them to the skillet, season with salt and pepper, and

cook for about 7 minutes or until the peppers are tender. Serve with tortillas and guacamole.

For the guacamole, finely chop the onion, tomato, and cilantro. Mash the avocado and mix in the remaining ingredients util well combined.

For the tortillas, mix the masa harina with water. Knead until the dough is soft and doesn't stick to your hands. Form walnut-sized balls and keep them covered with a damp cloth. Flatten each ball between two plastic sheets using a tortilla press. Place each tortilla on a hot griddle (comal) and cook for about 50 seconds per side, flipping twice. They're ready when golden spots appear. Keep the tortillas wrapped in a clean towel to stay warm and soft.

Chapter Eight

THE PROOF IS IN THE POT

Sheila Dene' Lawrence

The Rowsers enter a Chili Cookoff in an attempt to save their fledgling business. But what can save their struggling marriage?

Clues are sprinkled about; however, *The Proof is in the Pot*.

Ora stirred in the pot.

The heavyset cook replaced the lid before depositing the spoon in its ceramic cradle and wiping her tomato-stained hands on the flared skirt of her 'kiss the cook' apron. Turning, she met the watchful glare of her personal sous chef, Paul, who was slightly taller and substantially thinner; although, he was starting to show the early stages of a middle-age spread around his midriff.

With a peacock-like grin, she announced, 'I do believe this is the best batch so far, Hon. It's sure to be a strong contender in the cookoff today. Taste it and see what you think.'

Unsmiling, Paul harumphed. 'You leave out that spice you tried to kill me with last time?'

Like a chastised adolescent, Ora dropped her head. She paused before she answered, 'Of course. And how was I to know you had such a severe allergy to that spice when you didn't even know ... until you almost went into shock.'

He gave a slight chuckle that sliced through his accusation; however, it did little to lighten the perpetual heaviness weighing in the air between them.

'Yeah, it tasted real good, until my throat closed up. So, you should use it.'

'Are you crazy?' Ora inspected Paul's body language to detect any hint of a joke.

He appeared serious as he went on to explain, 'I'm thinking it could push us over the top and win this thing.'

Ora's eyes widened. 'Really? But what about ...'

With a raised hand, Paul interrupted her before she could refuse. 'But nothing ... I'll just stay away from it, that's all.'

'If you're sure,' she hedged.

'Yeah, I really think it could be a game changer this time around.'

'Okay, I'll consider it, but I think it may be good enough as is.'

Like syncopated swimmers, they moved around their

compact kitchen, finishing up the last batch of test chili before the contest that could rescue their fledgling business and stave off their debtors, at least for a short spell.

Ora couldn't help but notice that Paul moved about like an extra in a zombie flick, as if he was totally unacquainted with joy or any similar emotions.

Softly, she said, 'This money business can't be the only thing that has you so down in the dumps. We've been here before, and we'll turn it around again this time, too. So, what else is going on with you?'

'Nothing,' he snapped.

Softening his tone a bit, he asked, 'You get the recipe cards done?'

'Sure. They arrived from the printer a few days ago. They look really nice, so I wouldn't want to mess them up by penciling in another ingredient. I told you they'd come, but you don't seem to pay much attention to anything I say lately.'

'That's cause you always flapping your gums.' He mumbled, but she heard him clearly.

She said, 'Funny, you used to like that about me. Now, you complain about everything I do.'

Ora watched closely as her husband appeared fidgety and uncomfortable around her - as if they were honeymooners, instead of fifteen-year veterans in the war of matrimony.

After observing a while longer, Ora said, 'What gives? Will you just say it? What's so hard to share with your wife after all we've been through as a couple?'

'Right. I guess there's really no good time to say this.' Paul blurted out, 'Truth is – I don't love you anymore, Ora.'

After a few minutes of inhaling and exhaling the satisfying aroma of the simmering chili, she said, 'Last time you said that, I thought I'd made it clear that if you repeated it, that'd be the last time for me to hear you tell me.'

'Yes, I understood.'

'And?'

'And I really mean it this time.'

'So, that's it. Blow off our marriage, abandon the attempt to save the diner with this cookoff - just call it quits?'

Ora braced as she asked what she wasn't sure she wanted to know. 'Is there someone else?'

The silence was deafening until Paul finally found his words.

Enunciating, he said, 'This has nothing to do with anyone else. It's just between us. And now that I've gotten it out, how about we table it until we get through this cookoff, so maybe we have something left of the business to split up?'

'You want me to just act like you haven't made a statement that's going to change my whole life? Sure. Of course. Whatever Paul wants, Paul gets.'

She rambled a few moments with a tone of facetiousness to veil her growing anger.

Turning her back to Paul, who remained quiet and sullen, she lifted her chin and stared through the kitchen window above the sink. She would miss this view – her most cherished, but she mentally began making plans for her next.

Once she was sure she wasn't going to burst into a fit of tears, Ora walked back to the simmering chili.

She stirred in the pot.

❧

Time passed, and when the alarm beeped, signaling time to go into action, they simply did it.

The carefully pre-planned schedule the Rowsers had concocted to pull off this event was self-ingrained, so they robot-ically began packing up all they needed to head to the cookoff.

Paul gathered the utensils and pots, an extra burner, and Styrofoam bowls.

Ora gathered the ingredients and recipe, potholders, and monogrammed towels.

They loaded up the van and rode in complete silence as Ora

stared out her window and caught every tear before a single one escaped the corner of her eyes. She would not give Paul the satisfaction of seeing her brokenness.

They unloaded everything and set up at their stations in reverse order of their steps performed to get from their kitchen to the cookoff venue.

Ora and Paul didn't fuss or even speak, but each went about doing the task they had become accustomed to performing whenever they cooked together.

Ora noticed they had an audience of one who was closely watching their every perfunctory movement; she also noticed Paul conspicuously pretending to not notice the watchman.

'Oh, my God,' she gasped. 'It's that hussy that's always in your face, isn't it?'

'Lower your voice,' he chided. 'She has nothing to do with this. I told you, it's between you and me and nobody else.'

Ora did lower her voice all the way back to mute. She had always been able to read Paul like a cliched phrase. Now, she was sure the steam from her nostrils was fogging up her glasses instead of the atmospheric change from entering the muggy dining hall.

Before Ora was set to begin, she heard a voice calling out to her.

Plastering as genuine a smile as she was able, she looked around to see her gal pal rushing towards her.

As if on autopilot, Jeannie Sawyer hugged her and began helping to unpack the remaining bins without any sort of invitation. Jeannie glanced sideways at her while they worked. When she began to smolder like a pot on the verge of boiling and could no longer contain her suspense, she said, 'Spill it, Girl. What's wrong?'

'Nothing,' Ora said and shook her head. 'Got my game face on. That's all.'

Jeannie shook her head harder. 'Not going for it. You can't fool me. Who fought Scott Macon on the playground in first grade for bullying you? You ain't fooling me. This, it's not about nerves. What's going on?'

Ora got a chuckle from that reminiscence.

She whispered, 'Not now. Please. I'll tell you in a few – when there's not so many eyes on us.'

'Oh, you know I don't care nothing 'bout that.'

'But I do. So, hold on.'

'It's Paul, isn't it? What'd he do this time?'

'I said, hold on, Columbo.'

'Ok, but if this has something to do with that lil young half-naked chick fluttering around in Paul's face, I can't wait. I'm already on it.'

'So, it's not my imagination? You noticed it, too?'

'Girl, everyone has. You may be the last. But just keep your head up and keep on acting like you're still in the dark and ... if you want, I'll trip her up and step on her next time she comes sashaying through here.'

Ora covered her pain with laughter. She said, 'While I do like that idea, just be cool for now and let's make it through this without incident. I need to win this thing without anybody getting arrested.'

The cowbell rang. The timer started. The cooks went into action. They had two hours to complete their culinary masterpieces.

Paul and Ora worked as if there wasn't a thick wall of dissension between them.

Every now and then, Ora glanced up to see Rosalyn keeping surveillance on them. She had heard about the woman's reputation, though it never occurred to her that her own husband would be lured into an adulterous web by the curvy vixen's feminine wiles.

Ora's anger swelled, but her emotions stayed in the shadows of her motions. She stirred the pot, determined she would not lose both the contest and the cookoff.

Her pot had a nice smolder going on when the timer expired and the announcer said, 'Times up. Spoons down.'

And with that, he sent the contestants away from their stations for the judging to begin.

During the break, Paul went one way and Ora headed over to join Jeannie. For one - she needed some friendly energy to rejuvenate her. It takes a lot out of a scorned woman to behave seemly, and for two - she didn't trust Jeannie's restraint to hold while standing in such close proximity to her recently discovered nemesis or to be near her spouse.

Ora sidled over to Jeannie, as if all was well with the world and she wasn't nervously awaiting her fate to be decided by a few chili-tasting judges.

'How do you think you did?' Jeannie asked, bouncy and expectantly.

'This recipe is one of the best, according to Paul. You know he loves my chili anyhow, but he did suggest I add a little something to push us over the top. I didn't add it because the recipe cards were already printed, but I'm starting to wish I had. Paul thinks it would have guaranteed us the win.'

'What is it? CBD oil or something?'

Ora swatted at her. 'No, silly. Of course not.'

'I'm just saying all of these are really good so what could be the pièce de résistance?'

'I'll tell you, but it stays here.'

Ora stuck her pinky finger toward Jeannie, who hooked hers around it and said, 'Pinky swear.'

'It's cumin.'

'Cu-who? I'm not familiar.'

'A spice that gives off sort of a nutty flavor that Paul just absolutely loves, and a lot of others agree.'

The duo overheard shuffling behind them. They turned in time to see the disturbance was none other than Rosalyn Moore, who had been posted up behind them and was now stumbling over someone else's husband while trying to sneak away from them.

'What the … ?'

'I'm on it,' Jeannie said and made a move to pursue.

Ora grabbed her arm. 'Not worth it. Was she snooping or what?'

'There's one way we'll find out. If she ever adds cumin to anything, she better know how to use Paul's epi-pens he keeps on him because there won't be time to wait for 911 to get there.'

'I don't understand.'

'Paul likes cumin, but it doesn't like him. He's severely allergic to it.'

Jeannie laughed until she doubled over and tears leaked from her eyes.

She said, 'Too bad she didn't hang around to hear that part. I think he's safe though because she doesn't look like cooking's her thing.'

A short time later, the culinary judges marched in, single file. The leader of the pack handed a sealed envelope to the announcer; it contained someone's next smile, perhaps, even their lifeline.

Being dramatic, the announcer paused for added effect; he fumbled opening the seal to reveal the winner of the prestige and the prize money.

Paul eased over to join Ora, who stood next to Jeannie holding hands and barely breathing.

Sounding like a boxing promoter, the judge said, 'And this year's chili bragging rights go to everyone's favorite couple, Paul and Ora Rowser.'

Paul and Ora turned toward each other and gave Oscar-worthy performances as they hugged and rejoiced – just enough but not too much.

'We won?' Ora gasped, 'I can't believe it.'

She clutched her cross-pendant dangling from her neck as

she breathed, 'Lord, give me strength' because, somehow, Miss Rosalyn had slithered up on Paul's opposite side to give him a congratulatory hug and whisper something in his ear.

Applying her invisible blinders, Ora held her peace and started toward the stage. Paul fell in tow behind her.

Taking the platform, the Rowsers joined hands long enough for a photo opp and to accept the grand honor. Paul took possession of the trophy; Ora took the check.

The announcer reminded the contestants of their final act of participation, which was to leave a prepared stack of recipe cards on the table for attendees so any having food allergies could be sure to avoid the contaminants that might trigger them.

He reminded the audience, 'Contestants are only required to share the ingredients but not any specific measurements for you to be able to recreate the exactness of their masterworks.'

He also announced, 'Bowls will be offered as long as the chili lasts, so get in line and select your choice.'

Jeannie hunched Ora when she saw Rosalyn pick up a recipe card from the winner's table. She jotted something on the card before stashing it in her back pocket. Her last act was to grab two bowls and disappear through a side exit.

Jeannie muttered in Rosalyn's direction, 'Good riddance, floozy.'

Turning to Ora, she said, 'Now, can we talk?'

Hesitating only slightly, Ora told her friend, 'Well, you might as well know, Paul and I are through. This was our final act.'

Jeannie said, 'Wow. And what a way to exit. What now?'

Ora exhaled as if she had been holding that breath for a beat too long.

'I'll probably go back to catering. I don't want the hassle of keeping the diner going on my own. And most of the recipes are mine anyway. This prize money, or rather half of it, will help the transition a lot.'

'You know I'm here for you - whatever you decide, right?'

'Good, then help me break this down and clean up. Seems my hubby has disappeared, again.'

Jeannie spoke with the calm of a therapist. 'You know, I'm not sad about this. You deserve better.'

She began grabbing utensils and said, 'Let's do this.'

Paul showed up in time to load up the bins the ladies had haphazardly packed. He announced he had something to do this evening so he would drop her off and keep going.

'Uh-huh,' was all Ora said.

Jeannie jumped in and volunteered, 'Don't bother. I can drop Ora off. Why don't you go ahead and do you?'

He accepted the offer by closing the door behind the loaded inventory and trudging away. If he said thanks, there were no witnesses.

En route to the Rowser's residence, the levee finally broke, and Ora's tears caused a flood. She cried all the way home.

Jeannie let her.

When they made it inside the home, Jeannie announced, 'That's enough. I got champagne. It's time to celebrate. You've won twice today.'

'I guess so. I knew I'd lost Paul emotionally for a while now.'

'Welp, he's good ole Ros' problem now.'

A faint smile crossed Ora's lips. 'Yeah, I should send her a 'thank you' or something.'

Jeannie grabbed a couple of fancy flutes. She knew Ora's dining room arrangement almost as well as its owner and decorator.

'No need to send her nothing. Her greedy self took two bowls of your prize-winning chili, That's all she gets.'

'Well, I hope she and whoever eats that second bowl both get gas, especially if it's my hubby.'

'That's more like it. Cheers.' Jeannie howled like a hyena, and Ora joined her as they clinked glasses.

Their lingering giggles almost drowned out Ora's ringtone; she composed herself before answering.

'Hello.'

Then, she listened, nodded her head for all of sixty seconds and asked, 'Where is he? I'm on my way.'

Jeannie's eyes asked everything her mouth didn't.

Ora answered, 'It's Paul. He's headed to the emergency room. Possible allergic reaction to something from somewhere - wherever he just had to go tonight instead of coming home.'

Stumbling, Jeannie rose to her feet. 'I'll send for a ride. Neither of us are in any shape to drive.'

While Jeannie typed away in the app on her phone, Ora busied herself during the wait. She needed something to fill the few minutes that seemed like an hour.

To expend the nervous energy, she scoured the cooking tools and loaded all things chili-tainted into the washer before she pressed the extra hot and extra rinse buttons.

No sooner than when the kitchen was devoid of all chili residue, did Jeannie shout, 'Ride's here.'

Grabbing her keys, purse, phone, and a heavy garbage bag filled with tin cans, empty containers, paper wrappers, fuzzy leftovers, injector cartridges and all food-related refuse that had been discarded that day, Ora raced out the door. She stopped at the dumpster and still managed to beat Jeannie to the backseat of the hired vehicle.

When the twosome arrived at the hospital, they spied Rosalyn through the plate-glass window; she was pacing in the waiting room.

Their unspoken words and sideways glances exchanged said it all. Their suspicions had been confirmed. Apparently, Paul had been celebrating with his girlfriend instead of his wife.

A detective, a doctor, and a chaplain met Ora at the check-in desk as soon as she told the receptionist her name.

Looking at the threesome, she thought – this has all the makings of the intro to a bad joke.

'What happened?' she asked, as she was led away to a quiet room with Jeannie on her heels.

The response was polite silence with half a smile accompanied by an outstretched hand gesturing for her and Jeannie to follow after the leader wearing the white jacket.

She leaned over and burbled to her confidante, who was sticking closely to her side, 'How many folks do it take to tell a wife her husband fell ill while cheating on her?'

After Ora safely settled onto the edge of a seat, the doctor on duty took center stage and began his spiel.

'Mrs. Rowser, I'm so sorry to inform you that we were too late to save your husband. By the time paramedics arrived, he had already succumbed to anaphylaxis.'

Ora did the best ever imitation of concrete while she listened. More than a few seconds lapsed before her mind grasped what her ears had heard.

She repeated to the air in between her and the closest person, 'Succumbed? Paul's dead? That can't be.'

The physician patted the top of her hand as it rested open and flat against her thigh.

'Yes, Ma'am. I'm so sorry.'

Turning only her neck to gaze upwards at the stranger, she said, 'Where is he? Where was he?'

The doctor stepped aside for the uniformed officer to take over the conversation from his vacated vantage point.

'Yes, Mrs. Rowser.' He whipped open a notepad and read, 'Approximately an hour ago, we were dispatched to a residence in the Green Meadows subdivision where we discovered a Mr. Paul Rowser. He was non-responsive with all the symptoms of someone suffering from anaphylactic shock. There was one person present at that time, and we have a statement from her that we can share – from a Miss Rosalyn Moore. Are you acquainted with her as well?'

'Yes, but apparently not as well-acquainted as my husband. I mean, I know who she is, but I have no dealings with her,' Ora's voice trailed off at the end.

'Yes, ma'am. I know this must be a shock and I'm profoundly

sorry for your loss. We'll give you this time to grieve, but as soon as you're up to it, we will need to ask you a few questions. It's just routine.'

Jeannie whispered, 'Can this wait? She's been with me at her own house all evening, so I don't know that there's going to be a lot she can tell you. He never came home after the chili cookoff.'

Meanwhile, Ora remained stoic and still. She was too numb to cry - yet. No one had punched her; however, she felt that initial impact of a lick that stuns and renders one utterly immobile until the brain catches up to react.

Slowly, warm, salty tears began to creep down Ora's cheeks, though she remained frozen in an objectless stare.

The doctor returned to take her pulse and check her pupils. He pressed his stethoscope to Ora's chest.

'I agree. It'll have to wait.' He propped up Ora's feet and legs. He reclined her seat.

'Just breathe for me, Mrs. Rowser. Deep and even. Slower.'

He motioned for a nurse and mouthed, 'Shock.'

The nurse scurried away.

When Ora awoke, the first person she saw was Jeannie looming over her.

She said, 'Hey, Girl. Don't ever scare me like that again.'

Ora nodded, and that was the last recollection she had until the following day when her first visitor in the hospital room was the detective who had delivered the news that Paul had made her a widow.

'Sorry, we can't wait any longer,' he said. 'The first twenty-four hours are critical and we're already past that, so we need to ask ...'

'Wait. How long have I been here? What day is it?' Ora talked over him.

She was more interested in how many days she had missed than answering questions about a cheating spouse who lost a fight with an allergy foe.

Once Detective Eldridge Hanes properly introduced himself

and brought her up to date on day number two since Paul's demise, she agreed to answer his concerns.

'Ms. Moore says Mr. Rowser became ill immediately as he was eating chili you had prepared. Was there any ingredient in the pot not on this card she gave me?'

'No. Once the card was printed, I could only use those ingredients for the chili entered in the cookoff.'

'Do you have any chili left that we might evaluate?'

'It's all gone. Was there none left in the bowl Paul was eating?'

'Yes, and that is why we need to determine if the allergen was in the batch you prepared or whether Miss Moore intentionally added something before serving it to your husband.'

'So, that answers my question as to why a detective's asking questions about a man who obviously died from an allergic reaction? You think it was intentional? Like ... murder?'

'We just have to make sure it wasn't, Mrs. Rowser. Did Mr. Rowser have any enemies?'

'Don't we all?'

The detective sighed heavily. 'Anyone that might want to see him dead?'

'No, most folks liked Paul a lot, except perhaps my friend, Jeannie. But she was with me all evening. We were drinking champagne and celebrating my win.'

'Do you have the pot used? Has it been cleaned yet?'

'Everything's been scoured, scrubbed, and scalded. To prevent permanent stains, I do that as soon as possible.'

'What about the garbage?'

'Emptied and picked up.'

'So, all evidence of this batch is gone?'

'All gone. Since it won, we were the first table to run out.'

'Ironic, that it's called Killer Chili.' He seemed to be fishing, as it was more of a statement than a question.

'Even more ironic that Paul named it that,' Ora said, matching his vibe.

Ora couldn't tell if the officer's current pause was due to frustration or annoyance over this tic-tac-toe-like conversation, so she watched his every move for a clue.

'This is the card we got from Ms. Moore, and there was one handwritten ingredient on it that she says she got from you.'

'Impossible. I've never communicated with my husband's mistress.'

He showed her a picture taken of the card.

Ora grimaced, 'While that is my recipe card, that's definitely not my handwriting. It's barely legible.'

'Do you know what it says?'

'Yes, and since my husband has, or rather had a severe allergy to cumin, I wouldn't have added that to my recipe or served him anything with it in it. We found out quite by accident the first time I cooked with it. I chucked the rest of that brand new bottle, but he was understandably paranoid after that. He would sometimes watch me cook. Even went and got some of those shots he carried around with him all the time - just in case he ran into more surprise allergies.'

'If he'd had one of those shots, he'd still be with us. That's what's confusing. He had a case, but no pens in it. Miss Moore stated that he seemed genuinely surprised when he saw the case was empty. She states he pulled it out once he realized he was having a reaction.'

'Hmm, that makes no sense. Could anyone else have emptied it?'

'There were no prints other than his on it. And even though Ms. Moore gave a lot of conflicting information, we have no choice but to close this investigation as a no-fault death incident.'

'I'm curious. What else did Miss Moore have to say?'

'Plenty. She first claimed she'd made the chili. But then she admitted, you made it, and she only put it in a pot to warm it up. Then, when we found traces of cumin, she said you told her to add it. And when we asked, when was that, she confessed that you had not directly spoken to her, but she actually overheard you tell someone else. She, lastly, said you tricked her into killing your husband because you'd discovered that he was leaving you for her.'

'That's absurd. I only found out about her while she was stalking us at the cookoff.'

Ora had gotten loud and animated with her last reply.

The doctor stepped in and brought a halt to the interview.

'That's going to be enough for now, Detective. She's just coming back from a pretty bad case of shock. So, maybe hold off until later today?'

'Sure. I can do that.'

Then, he half-joked when he said, 'Keep an eye on her until then, Doc. Okay?'

Ora reassured him, 'I'll be here. I don't know where my clothes are stashed.'

The doctor closed the door as they both left.

Once outside the room, he asked the detective, 'Why all the questions? Do you actually think the wife had something to do with the death?'

Detective Hanes admitted, 'I think she did, but without anything less than a signed confession we have nothing tangible to prove it. Unfortunately, both she and the mistress will likely go scot free because there's no real intent or motive with the girlfriend and no real proof or opportunity with the wife. The Killer Chili could have proved it, but it's all gone. The proof was in the pot.'

BIO:

When she is not writing cozy mysteries, Sheila Dene' Lawrence can be found problem-solving as a Systems' Analyst or soul-saving as a licensed, ordained minister. She makes her home in Birmingham, Alabama.

RECIPE

Killer Chili

Prep Time 15 minutes
Cook Time 45 minutes
Total Time 1hour
Servings: 8 servings

Ingredients
2 pounds lean ground beef
1 onion, diced
4 cloves garlic, minced
2 ½ tablespoons chili powder, divided, or to taste
1 teaspoon cumin
1 green bell pepper, seeded and diced
1 can Rotel
1 can light red kidney beans drained and rinsed
1 can dark red kidney beans drained and rinsed
14.5 ounces canned petite diced tomatoes with juices
1 ½ cups beef broth
1 cup beer
1 small can tomato paste
1 tablespoon brown sugar
salt and black pepper to taste

Method
Combine ground beef and 1 ½ tablespoons chili powder.

In a large pot, brown ground beef, onion, bell pepper and garlic.
Drain any fat.
Add the remaining ingredients and bring to a boil.
Reduce heat and simmer uncovered 45-60 minutes or until chili
has reached desired consistency.
Optional toppings: sour cream, cheese, cilantro, tortilla strips,
chives. Serve with cornbread.

Chapter Nine

DEATH BY DAL

Shana Frost

Billy knows what he saw: a dead body. But by the time he called the police, the body was gone and all that remained was a container of takeaway Dal. Investigative Journalist Nina Banerjee is interested in this bizarre case and so is her Private Investigator boyfriend Robert Muller.

Did Billy hallucinate on that foggy winter's night or were there more sinister secrets at play? Nina and Robert must start with Dal.

Nina

'That's when I saw it - the container of dal.' Billy's shoulders drooped, just like his waning hope.

Nina had vowed he would not end up back in police custody. She dug the nib of her pen into the paper. Not only had she failed, but they were also none the wiser about what had happened.

She sighed. 'Let's try again, shall we?'

Billy shrugged as if his hope was draining fast. For several years now, Billy had worked hard to renew his life, starting with staying away from a life of crime. But now...

'On December 15th, you shut the pub and headed back home. Only as you neared the back door, you saw a pair of feet sticking out onto the pavement. You went to investigate and found it was a man... with no pulse. So, you called the police and all they found was a container full of dal?'

Billy scrubbed a hand over his face. 'Aye, and they arrested me for "stealing" Samuel Page's wallet. I only took it out to identify who he was.'

Nina flashed her teeth. She knew from experience how difficult things got when the evidence lied, and the cops trusted it. 'You then contacted Mr Page, who didn't answer. So, we know the body you found was him - only, *it* is missing, inconveniently.'

'Conveniently.' Billy shuddered. 'Imagine if they actually found him. That would seal me shut in my cell forever.'

Nina rubbed her forehead. This incident had taken place a fortnight ago. Now with Christmas behind them and Hogmanay around the corner, Billy had missed spending the holiday with his son, whom he'd recently reconciled with. All because he'd been trying to help a dead man.

Nina reached out and patted Billy's hand. 'We will get you out, trust me.'

Even if, with each passing day, she too lost faith.

When Nina left the prison thirty minutes later, she headed into Glasgow's City Centre. After they had met and solved a case together in the City Centre, she and her boyfriend had rented out a flat there. It was expensive, but it was also, very weirdly, sentimental. Besides, they ran their wee businesses from the flat.

Before she turned the key in the door, the aroma hit her. Dal... And then she saw him, barefoot in the kitchen, red splotches on his pale face and the dark blond hair sticking out. The man even wore an apron declaring him: "World's Best Scran-*bai*". The man had customised it and used it every time he cooked.

She took a moment to roll her eyes, then asked, 'What are you doing?'

The kitchen was a mess. A stainless-steel utensil containing yellow liquid burbled on the hob, and around it was utter mayhem. Onions, ginger and a packet of thin green chilli lay scattered across the chopping board. Robert had knocked over the container of red lentils, and some of the grains had landed right into the jar of turmeric powder he'd left open.

And he was chopping garlic on a steel plate... Then, 'ouch.'

Nina peered over his broad shoulders. Ah, he'd nicked himself on his left forefinger. He stuck the digit into his mouth and made a face.

The man was all corded muscles and strength. Heck, he'd broken his thumbs to get out of handcuffs to protect her. But small nicks like this?

Nina pulled his finger out of his mouth, stuck it under the tap, then picked up the jar of turmeric powder and dumped some on his finger. 'Turmeric doesn't scar. And clots the blood.'

He winced, then watched the yellow power turn orange. 'Thanks. I was, er, wondering if dal was the answer, you know.'

Nina narrowed her eyes, then spotted the notebook sitting right next to the hob. When they had visited India a few months ago, so she could get reacquainted with her family, her mother had tried to teach her to cook. At the end of their three weeks,

Nina still couldn't differentiate asafoetida (*hing*) and black salt. So Robert had swooped in. After some really nasty mornings spent sweating and crying in the kitchen, the man now didn't just cook, he made chapattis. Perfectly round, soft and edible chapattis.

How is cooking the dal going to help?'

Robert waved his hand towards the coffee table in the living room. Their wee flat was compact enough that the kitchen sat at the end of their living room.

Nina stepped away from the kitchen. Most days, her mere presence near uncooked food sent something burning. But God, Robert needed a job, even a small gig that got him back to work. Ever since he had quit the police force to become a private investigator, he had taken up half of their dining table and the entire kitchen table.

He cooked Indian meals using homemade recipes from her mum's book: poha, dal, rice, gravy... She appreciated him trying to keep some parts of her culture with her, she truly did, but heck. All that mess in the kitchen was just the outward reflection of his own mind.

Nina touched the laptop's mouse and brought the screen to life. It showed an image of a couple with their heads pressed together. She frowned. 'Who is this?'

'Proof that Becker is a philanderer.' Robert swiped the knife he was holding. 'See the other desktop screen.'

Nina swooshed her fingers over the trackpad and pulled up the second screen Robert had been working on. It was a website of a company called Khana Foods, and it showcased some really interesting and difficult to find Indian spices: special sun-dried chilli, homemade ghee, authentic garam masala, tamarind slabs, *Kokam,* and other niche products.

Oh god, was he buying more food? 'They sell these by the kilo. That's too much for just the two of us.'

Robert plopped some of the cut veggies into the pot and

stirred. 'I wasn't thinking of purchasing that, your mum sent some with us, remember?'

Hard to forget when Nina had been stressing about border control asking them why they had 2 kgs of thin white powder in their bags. Apparently, special *chakki-atta* (wheat flour made in a special crusher) made the best chapattis.

Nina rolled her eyes. 'Why are you researching Khana Foods?'

'Check their sales team.'

She scrolled over to the appropriate page, then frowned at the long list of names and faces. They clearly had a huge team around the UK, and a range of local suppliers in the Indian subcontinent. Nina still couldn't figure out why Robert had pulled this page up, but then she saw it... Khana Foods had a sales team made up of a local marketing team as well as a team that was always on the go, speaking to suppliers and doing research. And the part of the travelling salesperson team was a Samuel Page - their Samuel Page.

'We found him,' Nina whispered.

Robert set the lid on the burbling dal. 'Aye, we did.'

Robert

Robert rested his elbow on the table, frowning at the papers sprawled around the tiny dining room/work table, the phone pressed against his ear as he took down notes.

When he wasn't out investigating philanderers and con artists, he used this place to collate data, do admin for his new business, and send out the all-important reports and invoices. But when Nina decided to work from home too, their flat felt smaller than it already was.

He loved his girlfriend, but they were opposites in many

ways. For one, she loved emailing her leads, and he loved talking on the phone.

'Hm... hmm.' He nodded.

Nina shot him a glare.

He shrugged. 'Aw, that's truly heartbreaking. He sounds like a man who had so much potential.'

'Oh yes, he did,' the voice on the phone said. Betty was the receptionist at Khana Foods. Her posh accent came with a tight upper lip, but when he'd mentioned she was the one who knew how things worked in their office, she had thawed and was now in the process of explaining the office rumour chain to him. He knew about the top dog Amit Narayan. And he knew about the board. But most importantly, he knew about Samuel Page and his team.

The man had never married, being committed to his job in finance, before he'd had some sort of a stress breakdown and quit. This travelling job at Khana Foods took him around the country and sometimes to the EU. Apparently.

'It was the easiest job he's got. But I suppose he had the travelling bug, you know? I always told him he should visit India, and he'd finally get his dal fix.'

Robert smiled. 'I've been and I will say, it's the best food I've ever tasted.'

'It wasn't just any food he wanted. though.'

'Oh?'

For a woman who had almost hung up on him when he'd first called, she sure had the gift of the gab. 'Och aye, he loved to travel, but it wasn't just any travel. Mr Page was obsessed with dal, almost stalked it, like. He'd ask me to find him a hotel near some new dal place. It could've been research, but it was something else, it had to be. It's a bit nuts, isn't it, to change your itinerary and hotel stay to fit where you get the best dal in that city?'

It was, but that told him a few things about Samuel. Robert asked a few more follow-up questions. With each growing minute, he could feel the intensity of Nina's glare growing more smouldering. When she all but reached across the desk to smack the phone away from his hand, Robert finally said goodbye to Betty.

'One hour. Who is she? Your new tea party pal?'

Robert shrugged. 'I could take her to tea, honestly. Her intel has the potential to throw this case wide open.'

Nina folded her arms, staring at him as if she expected him to elaborate on that statement. Robert stared at his notes. 'Samuel Page. Late forties, single, never married. Ex-financier, now travelling salesman. Dal aficionado.'

'And how does that "throw this case wide open"?'

Robert smiled. 'Samuel Page loved his dal. But not just any dal, he loved onion dal.'

Now Nina's eyes gleamed, 'That's a strange preference for dal. Not something you commonly find in restaurants here.'

Robert nodded. 'Every time Betty booked a hotel for him, he would make sure it was near the place he wanted to try out. And guess what he ordered when he was in the office for lunch?'

Nina snatched the paper Robert had been scribbling on. 'Unmarried - and your notes say he didn't have family. So, whoever killed him knew about his obsession with dal - or onion dal.'

Despite his years on the police force and his new private investigation gig, death by dal was one of the strangest things he had ever dealt with. The strangest being falling in love with the woman he'd been sure was a criminal.

The woman now currently stabbing away at her laptop's keys, eyes the brightest they had been these last few weeks.

Nina

Nina sniffed the air. The smell of wafting spices engulfed her in its warm embrace. Wandering around on this rain-drenched Hogmanay day, that aroma at least meant she was in the right place.

She stared at the Maps app on her phone. Billy had found Samuel Page on this street. She tried picturing her surroundings in complete darkness, as it might have looked that night. She didn't have to stretch her imagination too far - it was winter, and this was Glasgow.

And on this damp day, the raindrops made up for the wintery fog that had prevailed the night of the 'discovery'.

Nina turned around to squint at the spot Billy said he'd spied the man and then the dal. She sniffed the air again. To be able to smell spices when it rained during winter meant she had to be close to the source.

Since Robert's discovery of Sam Page's love of onion dal, Nina had asked him to follow up with his new pal. And this time around, Robert had extracted the image of a handwritten onion dal recipe, as well as an entire list of places Samuel had eaten or wanted to eat dal. The man had the most hole-in-the-wall spots picked across the UK.

Finally, as she walked underneath a bridge near the High Court, the map pinged. Ah, there it was. Dal-Housie. Wow, this dal place Samuel had gone looking for was literally situated in a crevice created by the ground and the bridge overhead.

And there was a queue of people waiting. In this weather. In any other circumstances, Nina would have licked her lips. But after the cooking-spree her boyfriend had been on for the last month or so, Nina just couldn't bring herself to drool. She'd had her fill of dal-tadka.

Still, she queued up. Over the years, she'd learned that if she showed interest in her leads, they reciprocated.

Besides, queuing gave her the opportunity to stare into the shop without it looking weird.

She noticed a couple of things before they had served the person at the till. The place did take-aways only. And their menu had two dal varieties on the menu - plain dal or dal-tadka. And both were served with a heap of rice and pickles.

The queue moved up and, surprise-surprise, Nina's mouth watered. Her stomach let out a growl. She touched it then started mentally listing more observations.

Most people in the queue were South Asian, at least ethnically. Seeing a restaurant frequented by people who knew a thing or two about the cuisine was always a good sign of its authenticity.

There were two servers inside, one packing up orders, the other collecting the cash. The man dishing up the food was much smaller than the cashier, his white clothes reflecting in the light the only sign he was even in there.

Her stomach growled again. The fact that she was salivating over the food despite her own flat smelling like a *dhaba* for the last two months meant the food had to be amazing.

The queue moved up, and the person in front of Nina placed her order. 'Two plain and one tadka. I don't need all that rice, though.'

No sooner had she tapped her phone to the payment device than the packed containers sat in a white plastic bag waiting for her to pick up.

Wow.

Nina pulled her phone out when it was her turn. 'I didn't know you served dal here.'

The man behind the counter, compared to his colleague, was tall and bulky. He took up most of the small space, aside from the large containers of dal in the back. And based on his raised eyebrows, he clearly wasn't a fan of words.

'Er... plain dal and dal-tadka?'

He grunted, and in the next second there were two steaming containers on the counter.

Not wanting him to hurry her along, Nina thrust her phone into his face. He jerked back, knocking his hand against the container of dal tadka. Some dal splashed onto the counter.

'Have you seen this man?' Nina squeaked. Had she also lost all tact? 'Sorry, it's just that he told me he'd eaten here, and you know... I don't believe he'd stomach the dal-tadka. Me? I'll be fine. But this dude?'

His response was another glare as he mopped the spilt dal.

'Look, this is important. We have a bet going on, and my ego's on the line. You have to—'

He placed a lid on the container and smashed it into place with a loud crack.

'You know, your dal smells incredible. My boyfriend's been trying to make Indian food the entire month, and I thought I'd have my share, but this? It truly reminds me of home.'

The man ignored her, instead keying in the amount she owed into his payment device.

Nina took a deep breath, then caught the name tag on his uniform. 'Prakash, please, this is important.'

'Few weeks ago,' was his grunted response. 'He bought both dals and was happy with himself.' Then he thrust the payment device in her face, almost smacking her with it.

'Hey.' Nina massaged her jaw. 'What was that for?'

Someone tapped her on the shoulder. 'You're holding up the queue.'

Nina shot the customer a glare over her shoulder, then noticed the queue had indeed built up. It snaked all the way from Dal-Housie to the donut place two doors down.

'Did you see him eat the dal?'

Prakash once more thrust the device at her. 'Pay now.'

Nina tapped her phone to it to make the payment. 'Please?'

'No.' He curled his lip. 'I was busy.'

She opened her mouth to ask if Samuel Page had been with

someone that night when the customer behind her shoved her to the side. Rude.

And Prakash turned to his new customer.

Great.

Nina plucked her dal containers from the counter, then stalked towards Billy's pub. Cars zipped alongside the road. But this time of the year, the road got quite dark. It ran between a car park, two buildings and a bridge.

If something had happened here, that too on a foggy night, no one would have seen anything.

Nina huffed, then stared at the dal. 'You better have some answers for me.'

&.

Robert

As a cop, he had done interviews before. Had even been taught how to interview people of interest. But this... 'How do we interview a dal?'

Nina sat in front of him on the table. They had cleared it of papers and devices so they could use it for its original purpose: dining.

Only they weren't eating the dal. No matter how much its aroma tugged at his stomach - despite the jealousy that stirred in his gut, given his girlfriend had cheated on his cooking with restaurant food - Nina had prevented him from eating both varieties.

She had taken photographs, *lots* of photographs, in various angles. Then sniffed both dals, before scowling at them.

'I'm hungry,' he said, reaching for the cutlery he had placed on the table before she had crushed his dreams and let the steamy dal-rice grow cold.

Nina frowned. 'We have leftover dal, don't we?'

Seriously? She wanted him to eat leftovers, but she would eat this? He certainly enjoyed his cooking, but dal always tasted best when it was fresh. 'We could share.'

Grumbling at him, Nina stood up and headed into the kitchen.

Robert reached for the spoon and—

'Drop it or I will chuck this bottle at you.'

'I'm hungry.'

But his repeated pleas and demands fell on deaf ears. Nina set the leftover dal in the microwave and set the timer to six minutes.

'Two and a half,' Robert called out. 'Please don't burn it or the flat down.'

How had this woman survived on her own for fifteen years?

'Ha, ha,' was her retort, completely devoid of any glee.

He watched the two dals in front of him, then the one going in circles inside the microwave. His stomach let out a groan.

The microwave beeped, and finally Nina placed the leftover, now steaming, dal in front of him. Robert grabbed it and the spoon at the same time and dug in. Before she got any other ideas... 'Hum.'

Nina shoved the fresh plain dal at him. 'Now eat this.'

He narrowed his eyes, then dug into the new one. 'Oh god. *This* could have killed him easily. It's sooo good.'

'Try the dal-tadka.'

He did her bidding, then frowned. 'It's... okay? I mean, it's too salty. Taste it.'

Nina took a bite from the tadka, before trying the plain dal again. Her face twisted into a frown.

But when Robert picked up his spoon to take another bite, the plain dal container moved away and was replaced by the laptop. 'Why?' Robert pouted. But Nina wasn't in a mood to argue or eat.

She scrolled through the laptop, studying Samuel's dal-places document Betty had sent through. What had surprised Robert from that list was Samuel's meticulousness. He hadn't just listed out the places he wanted to try out, he had even listed out the name of the dal.

Nina waved at it. 'He had them in an order. All the places he had eaten at are up on the list and the pending ones further down. He's crossed each of them including *Dal Housie-Dal-Tadka.* But guess what the shopkeeper told me? Samuel Page ordered both dals from their menu. So why didn't he cross *Dal Housie-Onion Dal* from the list?'

Robert drummed his fingers on the table. 'Maybe he tried the dal-tadka and found it too salty? So he didn't bother with the other one?'

Nina pulled up the Dal-Housie's social media page next. 'He clearly was on a quest to find a dal that met with his former neighbour's recipe. So all the list of places he's ticked off do not meet the recipe. But... what if the onion dal at Dal-Housie did?'

'Why would someone kill him over it?' Robert sat back, staring at the plain dal. 'And besides, there is one mistake on Samuel's list. He had *Dal-Housie-Onion Dal* written on his list. But you just said they only do a plain dal and a dal-tadka.'

Nina showed him the social media pages she'd been studying. 'They do only serve two dals. But before Billy found Samuel Page, Dal-Housie had an onion dal and dal-tadka on the menu. There is no plain dal. In fact, they replaced it, and here in the reviews, people are complaining about it.'

Oh god. 'So he found the onion dal... and they what? Killed him over it?'

Nina smiled. 'Guess we will be finding out soon...'

Nina

The sun had called it a day, leaving Glasgow's streets dark and damp. And in this frosty weather, cold enough to leave behind black ice, still Nina hurried, not caring if she face-planted onto the pavement.

Robert jogged to keep up with her power walking. 'Are you sure we shouldn't call for backup?'

She had a hunch at this point, not solid evidence with which the police could do anything about Dal-Housie. Before they'd left the house, she had done a quick search on the business. Prakash Pinge had started it up right after his father's demise. Ever since, they had served customers two types of dals, each a homemade recipe. Only, since 15th December, the onion dal had fallen off the menu.

Nina led Robert to the bridge, careful of the sleet of ice formed near the shop. At this hour, the queue had vanished. It was officially too cold and too dark to operate in that wee spot.

Still, a van idled by the shop front, its back open and loaded up with empty containers. Nina saw Prakash hefting more boxes into the van. 'You don't make the dal here, do you?'

He jerked, almost skidding on a stray block of ice, then turned around. 'You again?'

Nina waved at the silent alley. 'And no queue to hamper our conversation. So it gives you enough time to confirm what I'm about to say.'

His eyes tracked over to where Robert stood beside her. 'Who are you? Reporters?'

'Tell me, Prakash.' Nina took a step closer. 'Why did Samuel Page and 5000 others like your onion dal? That dal-tadka we tasted was absolutely shite.'

'Don't know why you're obsessed with my dal, lady. It's personal choice.' Nina grinned up at Robert. 'Why don't we try the onion dal? We can make our choice then, can't we?'

'Would love to.' Robert frowned. 'But I can't see it on your menu.'

The shopkeeper crossed his arms, his eyes flitting between the two of them. 'What's your problem?'

Nina stepped closer, knowing she had hit a nerve. If she continued to press, he would explode. 'The onion dal wasn't on your menu after that night, was it?'

She pulled up her phone and showed him the reviews of his listing. 'And see the reviews. That onion dal was a fan favourite. Only... It's no longer on the menu. Apparently, you made the change the morning after Samuel Page was killed.'

Prakash's eyebrow twitched. 'I changed the menu because I wanted to. And I don't know this Page fella.'

'Don't you?' Robert moved closer to the man. 'You do realise in today's world our connections are easier to dig up, don't you?'

Prakash took a step back. 'I don't—'

'I asked you,' Nina picked up the thread. 'Whether Samuel Page had bought dals. Why did you lie?'

'I didn't lie,' Prakash shouted. 'He bought them both, but he didn't need to. He knew. Of course, that eejit knew.'

'You stole the recipe, used it to make this wee shop.' Nina stuffed her hands in her pockets. They had him now. 'And Samuel Page - he went searching until he found you.'

'That recipe was meant to be mine. It's my family's recipe. But my father gave it to that man, like he had any value for it.' Prakash stabbed his chest. 'My mother's family brought it with them when they moved to this country. It was mine to do with as I pleased.'

'And if Samuel would have taken you to court for it or asked you to pay a commission for its use, you'd have lost thousands. Your wee shop here is busy. This...,' Robert gestured to the wee shop. 'Makes you look authentic. And has cheap rent. Very little overheads. But it doesn't mean this place isn't as, or even more lucrative, than the restaurants on Ingram Street.'

Just when they expected Prakash to slump and give in, he

moved. In the blink of an eye, an empty container came flying at Nina. She shrieked just as Prakash leaped into the back of his van, more containers tumbling out as he went.

Oh god. He was going to jump into the driver's seat and hurry off.

Robert ran to the front.

'He's going to drive,' Nina shouted.

But her boyfriend didn't jump in to disarm the man. He simply laughed when Prakash landed in the front seat and fumbled for the keys. Robert raised his arm. 'Searching for this?'

In his hand was a set of keys.

'I wasn't born yesterday, pal.' Robert reached out and opened the door. 'Get out, hands behind your back.'

Then to Nina, Robert winked. 'I think we're better suited to being out in the field than cooped up at home, don't you think?'

She rolled her eyes, already dialling DI Cheryl Spiers, Robert's pal and their police contact. 'Hey, I've got someone I think you should meet.'

&

Robert

Robert watched Billy laugh as he poured the drinks. He had been released from custody, his latest imprisonment wiped from the record with a 'we're so sorry' letter to boot.

They had also found poor Samuel Page's body in the Clyde, caught in a nook between the boulevard and a jetty. The man had been laid to rest, and Prakash caught for the murder.

So Billy was back, and the entire pub buzzed with the spicy scent of mashed neeps, tatties and a generous helping of Haggis. It was Burns Night after all. But for their Burns Supper, Robert had also supplied Billy his tried and tested version of dal, the way Nina's Mum had taught him.

Their fusion of a meal had gone down well with the folks. Billy had invited his friends and usual customers. All his clientele were familiar with the custody suite, but Billy invited them so he could help them change their own lives, just as he had.

Tonight's celebrations were for Billy's release and for Samuel Page, who'd had no one to miss or mourn him. Betty had travelled up for the celebration and was now laughing with Billy, their heads pressed together.

'That dal is the best I've ever eaten.' Nina elbowed him. 'Mum says she's proud of you.'

Robert grinned. They had visited Mumbai for Nina to mend her relationships with her family, but he had ended up gaining a family as well. As someone raised by a single mum with no other relatives, it had been a welcome change. 'You must've been bored eating my trial versions.'

'I was, but, Robert, I know why you took up cooking.'

'Duh, it was trying to impress your parents. Didn't you say, if the spouse can cook, they get bonus points?'

'That works more when it's the to-be-wife and not the husband. And it only works if they are thinking of getting married.' She made a show of studying her fingers. 'As far as I can see...' She wiggled them. 'There's an interim step between dating and marriage that is yet to be fulfilled.'

Robert rolled his eyes. 'I'll get right to it, ma'am.'

'See that you do.' Nina wrapped her hands around his arm. 'Until then, thank you for cooking me the dishes I grew up eating. It was nice to taste them, here in Glasgow, after a decade of missing them.'

'It's tasty food.'

'It's hard to cook. And you took the effort. Thank you.'

Robert smiled down at her. 'I love you.'

Nina shook her head. 'And I, you. Even though you love to yap with people you don't know.'

With a sigh, she looked at Betty and Billy. Robert laughed.

Aye, his and Nina's lives were like dal. Whether plain or with a tadka, they were always interesting.

BIO:

Shana Frost writes romantic mysteries as dramatic as the Scottish Highlands that inspire her.

Always infused with a wee dram of the Scottish landscape and culture, Shana's stories take readers from Glasgow's gritty streets to the enigmatic Highlands. She promises that when reading her stories, you'll be on the edge of your seat, falling deeper in love with the characters.

RECIPE

Onion Dal

Ingredients
1 Cup Toor Dal
1/2 Finely Chopped onion
Turmeric Powder
Chilli Powder
Karwari Sammar Masala (a special dried masala prepared in Karwari homes)
Dried Monkey Jack or substitute for Kokam Phool
Coconut Oil

Method
Boil toor dal and 1/4th chopped onion in a pot
Once the dal is cooked, add a teaspoons of chilli powder,
Karwari sammar masala and a pinch of turmeric powder.

Let the dal boil again as you stir out any lumps
Add two rinds of dried monkey jack (or Kokam Phool)

Prepare the Tadka
In a separate small pot, add two teaspoons of coconut oil
Add 1/4th finely chopped onions to the heated coconut oil
Let the onions fry until they are dark brown (be cautious that
the onions don't burn)

Mix the Dal
Add the tadka to the dal
Immediately cover up the pot of dal so that the tadka soaks into
the dal's flavour

Serve warm with steamed rice

Chapter Ten

LEMONS AND LIES

DK Snyder

Natalie, a professional baker, finds her life upended when she becomes a suspect in the murder of her disagreeable next-door neighbor. Using knowledge she's gained on the job, Natalie searches for clues to find the real killer and clear her own name. But beneath a thin veneer of suburban tranquility, deception threatens Natalie's quest to ensure justice is served.

When Natalie got home from work on Friday afternoon, her husband was replacing the old wooden mantelpiece above the fieldstone fireplace in their living room. 'Did you hear about Jim?' Harlan asked, setting down his saw. Sawdust mingled with the gray flecks in his dark hair.

'No, what now?' Natalie asked without enthusiasm. After a long workweek at Breaktime Coffee, she'd been looking forward to a glass of wine and some time in her garden. Not a discussion about Jim Dwyer, their obnoxious next-door neighbor.

'His body was discovered this morning near the pond.'

'What?' Natalie searched for sense in Harlan's words.

'He's dead.'

The empty plastic bakery containers Natalie was carrying hit the wooden coffee table with a clatter.

'Did he have a heart attack?' She pictured Jim red-faced and ranting about his pet peeves in their homeowners' association: noisy children on the sidewalks, sagging gutters on the clubhouse, the board's ban on doorbell cameras, and recently even Natalie's backyard garden.

'No,' Harlan said. 'Tori found him lying face-down with a gash on the back of his head.'

Natalie grasped a brimming built-in bookshelf to steady herself. 'Oh no, poor Tori.' Natalie's closest friend in the neighborhood, Tori lived with her family in a white Colonial next to the pond.

'Don't you mean poor Jim?' asked Harlan with a smirk. He'd often urged Natalie to ignore their neighbor's complaints, which she thought was easier said than done once he targeted her own garden.

Natalie remembered Jim's long-suffering wife. 'How's Julia?'

'Haven't seen her.'

Harlan reached into his pocket and handed Natalie a business card. 'A homicide detective went from house to house today asking about everyone's activities this morning. He'll come back to interview you tomorrow.'

Natalie studied the card: Detective Michael Ford of the Fairfax County police department. She sank onto the overstuffed couch as her mind registered the reality of the murder. 'Do the police think it's a robbery gone wrong?'

'Probably not,' said Harlan. 'Luis told me Jim still had his wallet and phone in his pockets.' Luis was a lawyer who lived across the street.

'How'd he know... never mind.' Ever since she and Harlan had moved to the Tranquil Oaks homeowners' association, a community of twenty-five single-family homes in Washington, D.C.'s Virginia suburbs, Natalie had grown accustomed to rumors, cliques, and nonstop gossip. Not that she minded gossip – running a coffee shop would be much duller without it – but even after living in Tranquil Oaks for two years, she still felt like an outsider here. And while she'd come to expect the association's arbitrary rules and the residents' petty feuds, she never expected a murder.

❦

The next morning, Detective Ford sat facing Natalie in her living room as they sipped from mugs of coffee. About a decade older than Natalie's forty years, the detective wore a button-down shirt and slacks with a badge clipped to his belt. A batch of scones Natalie had baked for Julia was cooling on the kitchen counter, suffusing the first floor with the sweet, earthy aroma of lemon and rosemary.

Detective Ford placed his mug onto the coffee table and opened a tan notebook. 'Your husband said you're a professional baker?'

'Yes. I co-own a small coffee shop called Breaktime Coffee in an office building on Corporate Drive.' While Natalie appreciated the regular schedule, the shop itself wasn't much larger than an office. She hoped to open her own bakery soon and was searching for a lively street location with ample seating and an on-site kitchen. She often daydreamed about what she'd name it.

'That's a nice short commute,' the detective said.

'Yes, a fifteen-minute drive.' Short commutes were rare in traffic-clogged northern Virginia.

The detective flipped to a clean page in his notebook. 'Where were you yesterday morning, let's say between 6:00 and 8:00 am?'

'Here at home, until I left for work.'

'Tell me about your morning.'

'I woke up early to bake, like every weekday morning. Yesterday I made blueberry muffins and lemon poundcake. Then at 7:30 I loaded the bakery containers into my car and drove straight to Breaktime Coffee.'

'Where was your husband during that time?'

'Here. Harlan had a day off work and was doing home repairs.' They'd bought their house in foreclosure – otherwise they never could have afforded it – and were slowly fixing it up.

'Did you see anyone in Tranquil Oaks besides Harlan yesterday morning?'

Natalie searched her memory, wrapping her hands around her warm mug. 'As I loaded my car, Julia pulled into their garage next door.'

'The victim's wife?'

'Yes. I think she'd been visiting her sister in Baltimore.'

The detective scribbled a note. 'How would you describe Julia Dwyer's relationship with her late husband?'

Natalie recalled the bickering she'd heard through open windows during spring and fall. 'They argued,' she said, 'but you never really know about someone else's marriage.'

'Did you see anyone else in the neighborhood yesterday morning, even in passing?'

She frowned in concentration. 'Paige Hixon zipped past me in her new Mercedes SUV.' Natalie pictured the shiny black behemoth barreling past her blue Prius.

'The president of the Tranquil Oaks board of directors?'

'Yes.' And control freak, Natalie added silently. If home-owners painted their house the wrong shade of neutral, let their grass grow too long, or drove too fast on their quiet street, Paige would accuse them of violating the rules of the association in which they were mandatory members. But Natalie wasn't surprised someone so image-conscious would flout the traffic rules to show off her new car.

'What can you tell me about the victim, Jim Dwyer?'

'He's – was – our next-door neighbor.' There was an awkward pause. 'To be honest, Jim complained all the time, especially if someone's house or the common areas didn't strike him as perfect. His complaints antagonized a lot of people here.'

'So I've heard,' the detective said. 'Tranquil Oaks seems far from tranquil.' He smirked as if he were the first person to say so.

Natalie didn't smile. 'We didn't know all that when we moved here, of course. We had no experience with homeowners' associations, but the pond and the clubhouse looked nice, and the dues seemed reasonable for their maintenance. But over time, the dues and the drama both escalated a lot.' Natalie even had suggested to Harlan making good on their sweat equity and moving elsewhere, but he opposed the hassle and expense of moving.

'To your knowledge, was anyone unusually angry with Jim Dwyer lately?'

'Nobody stands out.'

'What about the woman who found his body?' The detective checked his notes. 'Tori Sato. Did she have disagreements with Mr. Dwyer?'

'Tori? Probably fewer than most,' Natalie said of her friend. 'She's pretty easygoing.'

'How about you?'

'Me?' Natalie blinked.

The detective leaned forward. 'Did he aggravate you especially?'

'Not really.'

'Hmm. The neighbors told me Mr. Dwyer filed a complaint with the association's board about your garden.' The detective flipped pages in his notebook. 'He said he couldn't enjoy his own backyard because of 'the weed-infested overgrown jungle next door."

Natalie flinched. 'Jim was prone to hyperbole.' She wondered which neighbor, or neighbors, had pointed Detective Ford toward her.

'Is your garden important to you?'

'Yes. I love gardening, and I grow ingredients for baking. Now in June, I'm harvesting two types of berries, a half-dozen herbs, a few vegetables, and lemons from a potted tree that bears fruit when I move it outside in the summer sun. Bakery items taste far better with fresh ingredients.'

The detective flipped another page. 'After Mr. Dwyer filed his complaint with the Tranquil Oaks board, you filed one against him?'

'He didn't even deny it was his dog's... poop on our lawn,' Natalie said, wrinkling her nose and struggling to keep her voice level. 'He said it would enrich the 'weed-infested overgrown jungle."

The detective barely suppressed a grin. 'What's the status of the complaints?'

'Paige, the board president, investigated. She checked my backyard last week and decided some of my plants, including the lemon tree, weren't on the association's approved list.' Natalie frowned. 'Then she stepped in dog poop, screamed, and promised to fine both Jim and me for violating the rules.'

'Were you angry with Mr. Dwyer about the threat to your garden?' No longer jocular, the detective fixed Natalie with a piercing stare.

'Wait.' Natalie nearly choked on her coffee. 'You can't possibly think I'd be involved in Jim's death.'

'When people have conflicts, sometimes accidents happen.' The detective's tone was casual, almost soothing, but his eyes remained laser-focused on Natalie. 'Maybe there was an argument, and he tripped. Or maybe you felt threatened and defended yourself. If that's what happened, it's best if you tell me now.'

Natalie gasped. 'I had nothing to do with Jim's death.' She flushed and her voice rose as her disbelief flared into anger. 'I'm not a murderer,' she said, realizing a murderer would say the same. 'Jim picked fights with everyone in the neighborhood. Nobody liked him. You should read his posts in the Tranquil Oaks Facebook group.'

'I will.' The detective stood. 'Thank you for the coffee. If you think of anything else, please let me know.'

As soon as Detective Ford walked out, leaving behind a residue of tension like a garden slug trailing slime, Natalie reached for her cellphone and examined Jim's final posts in the Tranquil Oaks group. Besides insulting Natalie's garden, Jim accused Paige of 'flagrantly illegal corruption' for spearheading the board's latest dues increase, demanded Luis remove the red Washington Nationals baseball flag from his own front yard, lamented (with photos) the sagging gutters on the clubhouse, and blamed the 'no-show incompetent Virginia Expert Masonry' for not yet repairing the deteriorating brick path around the pond.

Harlan arrived home from the hardware store with woodstain and brushes. 'It smells great in here. Lemon?'

'Lemon-rosemary scones for Julia. I saved one for you.'

'Thanks.' Harlan took a bite on his way back from the kitchen. 'Mm, the flavor balance is perfect.'

'It's my new recipe.'

'The rosemary-leaf garnish is a nice touch, too.' Then Harlan glanced at Natalie's phone and scowled. 'Why are you reading that nonsense?'

'Someone told Detective Ford about the conflict between Jim and me.' She continued scrolling. 'I need to learn who else Jim complained about before everyone here gangs up on me and I get arrested.'

'I'm sure you're not a suspect in Jim's murder,' Harlan said in a calm voice, touching her arm. 'The police need to question everyone. They can check the CCTV at your office building to find out when you arrived at work yesterday morning, right?'

'The video wouldn't prove where I was beforehand.'

'We both know you were at home baking.' Harlan flashed a mischievous grin. 'If you'd left the house to kill someone, your blueberry muffins and lemon poundcake would have burned.'

'A spouse isn't a great alibi,' Natalie said, allowing a tiny smile.

'Look, Natalie, no rational person would believe you killed Jim. You didn't feud with him more than anyone else did, and you've never acted violent.' Harlan, an IT contractor for the federal government, often soothed Natalie's worries with his calm rationality. But she doubted everyone else in Tranquil Oaks was equally rational.

&

Natalie covered the plate of scones with saran wrap and walked next door. It was a hot June day, and the mid-Atlantic humidity frizzed her curly hair as she proceeded up the slate front walk past a lawn and hedges weeded, watered, and pruned to soulless perfection. As she stepped onto the porch, Luis, the lawyer from across the street, opened Julia's front door from inside and turned back. 'Again, you have my deepest sympathy,' he said before greeting Natalie and crossing the street.

'What lovely scones,' Julia said, touching a needle-like leaf.

'Rosemary for remembrance.' Natalie hadn't realized she'd been holding her breath until she exhaled with relief at Julia's unsuspicious welcome.

A miniature schnauzer barked and pawed at Natalie's legs with excitement. 'Quiet, Tucker,' Julia said, and the dog scampered to lie down in front of a sleek sofa. The living room (a mirror-image of Natalie's and Harlan's layout, with the fieldstone fireplace on the opposite wall) was decorated with clean-lined furniture and geometric artwork.

They sat across from each other, and Julia stared at her hands. 'I can't believe anyone would kill Jim,' she said, shaking her head. Her eyes were dry but were underscored by dark smudges of fatigue.

'It's horrible,' Natalie said. 'Do the police have any leads?' She couldn't help asking.

'They questioned me about Jim's difficulties with neighbors, so they must suspect someone in Tranquil Oaks.'

'Really?' Natalie's stomach dropped.

'I told them I was skeptical,' Julia said. 'I know Jim wasn't well liked, but I don't believe a small disagreement about landscaping or flags led to murder.'

Natalie nodded. 'That's a very good point.' Tucker trotted over and aimed his intelligent eyes up at Natalie, who reached down to pet the dog's salt-and-pepper fur. She didn't blame the dog for Jim's pooper-scooper misdeeds, after all.

'Jim had anger issues,' Julia said, 'and we argued, but he didn't mean most of what he said.' She rubbed her forehead. 'I wasn't such a good wife, either.'

Natalie's eyes widened. 'Oh, Julia, I'm sure that's not true.' She was startled by Julia's self-reproach but understood how shock and grief could manifest as guilt. She remembered what she told Detective Ford: You never really know about someone else's marriage.

❧

The board decided that proceeding with the annual Tranquil Oaks summer barbeque on Sunday wasn't in poor taste because Detective Ford was available to update the community on the investigation. Carrying a container of chocolate-raspberry brownies, Natalie walked a block with Harlan to the clubhouse beside the pond. Out front, her friend Tori slathered sunscreen on her squirming son before he took off running toward a group of kids at a nearby volleyball net. Harlan continued to the backyard to help grill hamburgers and hot dogs.

Natalie joined Tori in the dappled shade of a tall crepe-myrtle tree heavy with pink blooms. She opened her container. 'Brownie?'

Tori's kind eyes lit up. 'I love brownies, thanks.' Natalie was reminded why she liked Tori. She was one of those forthright people who said what she thought and showed her feelings on her face. 'Mm... raspberry filling. From your garden?'

'Picked today.'

'How's your search for a bakery location going?'

'Slowly.' Then Natalie turned somber. 'Finding the body must have been a terrible shock.'

'Yes, horrible.' Tori's face fell and she shuddered despite the heat. 'And now I feel guilty for snapping at Jim during last week's board meeting. He said I was a lazy treasurer and demanded an outside audit, but that's just the way he was.'

'I'm sure you were nicer than most of us,' Natalie said, 'and a fine treasurer.'

'I agreed to that thankless job only after no one else here volunteered.'

Natalie was more interested in the murder. 'Did you see or hear anything unusual before you found the body on Friday?'

'No. Jim marched past my kitchen window around 7:00, like he did every morning to check on the brick path around the pond.' Tori glanced over her shoulder, then turned back to Natalie with a quiet voice. 'Do you think his wife might have, you know, killed him?'

'Julia?' Natalie lowered her voice too and shook her head. 'I doubt it. She seemed shocked and exhausted yesterday.' But then she remembered how Julia had reproached herself and taken Natalie's innocence for granted. 'It's true she and Jim argued all the time. He must have been terrible to live with. And the spouse is always a prime suspect, right?' Now Natalie worried she'd delivered scones to a murderer.

Tori drew closer. 'Not to spread rumors, but I heard that Jim asked Luis for help revising his will to cut Julia out.'

'Really?' Natalie's eyes widened. If the rumor was true, then Julia had a financial motive to kill her husband. But as she'd told Detective Ford, Julia pulled into her garage at 7:30 on Friday morning. She wouldn't have stopped at the pond first, allowing anyone to place her car at the crime scene, but might she have walked there afterward? Natalie didn't know what to think.

A small group of neighbors strolled past them into the clubhouse, including board president Paige and her friend Sloane, a personal trainer who lived up the street.

'Can you believe Paige told me to repaint my mailbox?' asked Tori.

'Yup.' Natalie rolled her eyes and headed inside while Tori jogged after a runaway volleyball.

The clubhouse featured a spacious room on the main level, plus a basement level with children's videos and games. The main room was alive with conversation as the residents of Tranquil Oaks circulated or sat at two long wooden dining tables. No one seemed especially distressed by recent events, and snippets of chatter reached Natalie inside the front door: *so many enemies*; *bet the killer lives here; maybe arrested tonight?* Across the room, tall windows overlooked the backyard and the pond, which was surrounded by yellow crime-scene tape. Detective Ford leaned against a side wall and scanned the room, handcuffs looped around his belt.

Paige and Sloane, standing near Natalie and sporting tight athleisure with matching logos, glanced at her and leaned toward each other, whispering like conspirators. Natalie was pretty sure she heard the words 'complain' and 'garden.' She wondered whether they were assessing her odds of arrest or only judging her botanical farmers market t-shirt. She held out her container.

'Would either of you like a brownie?'

'Oh no,' Sloane said, drawing back in alarm. 'I don't do carbs.'

'Can you believe what happened to Jim?' asked Paige, waving away the brownies. 'I was downtown yesterday for a hair appointment and shopping in Georgetown. I was shocked, just *shocked* when I got home and heard the news.'

Sloane leaned toward Paige. 'Are those new earrings from Tiny Jewel Box?' Blue sapphires sparkled. 'They're gorgeous and match your eyes.'

'Thanks.' Paige flipped her long beachy waves, and new blonde highlights caught the light. 'I feel so, *so* sorry for Julia,' she said with a not-sorry expression. 'Don't you? Obviously, she won't come to this barbeque today.' The two friends began whispering again, reminding Natalie of twelve-year-olds in a school cafeteria.

She turned and threaded her way toward the dessert table that stood alongside one wall. As she dropped off the brownies, a prickling sensation crawled up her spine, and she swung around to find Detective Ford watching her with a fixed stare from a few yards away. Her stomach dropped as his suspicious line of questioning echoed in her mind: *Were you angry with Mr. Dwyer... maybe you felt threatened...* Natalie tried to appear casual despite her racing heart as she walked out the clubhouse's back door.

The evening sun was heavy and low over the backyard, the dinner rush was over, and people were moving inside to escape the mosquitoes. Harlan and Tori chatted near a children's play structure to Natalie's left, and she was about to join them when she noticed three graying men in cargo shorts standing to her right near the grill. While one checked his phone, the other two watched Luis amble inside wearing a red Nationals baseball cap. Then they shifted their gaze to the yellow crime-scene tape.

Natalie had learned important lessons from interacting with her customers at Breaktime Coffee; she knew when someone had a good story to tell, and she knew the old stereotype that men gossiped less than women was flatly wrong. Hoping for more information to identify the killer and clear her own name, Natalie crouched behind a tall stack of bagged mulch and listened.

'Do you think he was honest with the cop?' asked the man in the middle, holding a large grill brush. Natalie froze.

'Who, Luis?' asked the guy to his right, looking up from his phone. 'What do you mean?'

'You know how Julia supposedly stayed with her sister in Baltimore last week?' the first guy asked. 'But Drew saw her at Nationals Park on Thursday with Luis. Right?'

'Yup,' said the guy to his left, who must be Drew. 'Acting like they wanted to appear on the kiss cam.'

'Was the Phillies game on Thursday?' asked Phone Guy. 'What a rout.'

'Sure was.' Behind the mulch, Natalie slapped a mosquito then cringed at the sound, but the men showed no sign they'd heard.

'Luis should be the leading suspect.'

'He had a clear motive to get Jim out of the way.'

'Did Jim know about the affair?'

'No idea. He was such a nutcase.'

'Yeah. Maybe Julia could have tolerated him if he'd stopped talking trash like Natalie's 'overgrown jungle' and Paige's 'illegal corruption," Phone Guy read from his screen. The other two men snorted.

'He was right to complain about the dues increases, though.'

'True.'

'And the crumbling path around the pond. Who'd the board hire to fix it?'

Phone Guy scrolled. 'Jim called them the 'no-show incompetent Virginia Expert Masonry."

'Who?'

'I've never heard of Virginia Expert Masonry.' Drew pulled his own phone from his pocket. 'The board should have hired my company instead.'

'Your guys did a great job on my front walk.'

'Some contractors won't even show up for a quote anymore. Last month I called five roofers...'

The discussion moved on, but Natalie stayed frozen in place. Now that she knew about the affair, she realized it might explain why Luis was at Julia's house the previous day. She wasn't sure whether Luis killed Jim, or Julia did, or perhaps they acted together. She wondered if she should tell Detective Ford what she'd heard. Or if he'd think she was pointing a finger at others to try to deflect the blame from herself.

❧

As the sunset faded into darkness, everyone crowded into the clubhouse for Detective Ford's update. All the chairs were taken, so Natalie lingered near the back door between Harlan and Tori. The detective stood at the head of a table next to Paige, who quieted the room.

'This is a continuing investigation,' Detective Ford said. 'As you know, Jim Dwyer's body was discovered face-down near the pond on Friday morning with signs of blunt-force trauma to the back of the head. The medical examiner's report is pending. The forensics team is processing the evidence collected from the crime scene, including multiple loose bricks, one of which may be the murder weapon.'

'Have you found the killer?' asked a woman seated near the detective.

'We've identified several potential suspects. We're also investigating Mr. Dwyer's recent interactions to identify potential motives.'

'Do you think the killer lives in Tranquil Oaks?' asked Sloane, standing in front of Natalie and holding a plate of celery.

'We're looking into the possibility the perpetrator was familiar with Mr. Dwyer's usual morning routine.'

Sloane turned and stared at Tori, who reddened and frowned.

'Everyone knew about Jim's morning walks,' Tori said. 'That's when he took pictures of his concerns and posted them. Like the brick path around the pond.'

'Yeah,' called a voice from the middle of the room. 'Jim might still be here with us today if the 'no-show incompetent Virginia Expert Masonry' had fixed that path.'

A chortle rose nearby, followed by a plea to show some respect.

'About the path...' It was Drew from the grill.

'What about it?' asked the detective.

'Virginia Expert Masonry?' Drew looked at Paige. 'Is that who the board hired to fix it?'

'Yes,' said Paige. 'They'll be here next week. Unless the area is still a crime scene, of course.' She aimed a questioning glance at the detective.

But Drew had more to say. 'I don't think they'll be here next week, or any other week, because Virginia Expert Masonry doesn't exist.'

Next to Natalie, Tori's jaw dropped, and the blood drained from her face. 'What do you mean they don't...?' She cut herself short.

Natalie touched Tori's arm and whispered, 'What's wrong?'

'Nothing.' But Tori's hand shook as she drank from her bottle of lemon iced tea. The lemons on the label reminded Natalie of her lemon tree banned by Paige. And the lemon-rosemary aroma at home when the detective suggested she'd felt threatened. And the men facing the yellow tape and quoting

Jim's rants. She sensed the answer to the unsolved murder hovering an inch beyond reach.

'Are you trying to be funny, Drew?' asked Paige with narrowed eyes. 'Of course, our contractor exists.'

'Nope,' said Drew. 'I checked the state licensing website.'

'I won't listen to this nonsense,' said Paige, scanning the room. 'Why are we wasting time when we have a killer at large?'

'Right,' agreed Sloane. 'Let Detective Ford finish his presentation.'

As the detective asked anyone with more information to contact him, Paige maneuvered toward the back door.

And Natalie knew the answer.

She took a deep breath, stepped in front of the back door facing inward, and gripped both sides of the doorframe.

Paige sneered. 'Get out of my way, Natalie. I need to go plan my outfit for tomorrow.' Paige's stale perfume wafted between them.

'You won't need to plan your outfits,' Natalie said, 'when you're in prison for killing Jim.' A collective gasp filled the air.

'How dare you?' Paige's spittle sprayed Natalie's face.

The room buzzed with excitement at the unexpected drama. Harlan stared at Natalie, his brow furrowed with a mix of confusion and concern, while Tori's eyes widened with dawning realization.

Detective Ford pounded the table to quiet the crowd and glared at Natalie. 'What's the meaning of this?'

'Paige killed Jim on Friday morning,' Natalie said in a firm voice, 'then sped out of Tranquil Oaks at 7:30 to spend the rest of the day pampering herself.'

'I don't know what you...' Paige scowled before rearranging her expression into innocent outrage and pivoting to face the crowd. 'That's ridiculous slander.' Her blue eyes blazed. 'I had no reason to want Jim dead.'

'Yes, you did,' Natalie said, arms still wide against the doorframe. 'Jim got one thing right, Paige: your corruption. When he demanded an outside audit, you felt threatened with exposure. Our homeowners' dues probably helped pay for your new SUV. And maybe those new earrings, too.'

'That's crazy.' Paige's hands rose to her earlobes. 'You have no proof.'

'Check the Tranquil Oaks financials,' Natalie said to Detective Ford. 'I bet you'll find a so-called deposit to a fictitious contractor. And who knows how many other suspicious payments.'

Paige's gaze darted over the rapt onlookers. She drew her shoulders back, stepped away from Natalie, and steadied her voice. 'Natalie concocted that preposterous story to hide her own guilt,' she said with a hand on her breastbone. 'Everyone knows Natalie was furious, just *furious* at Jim for complaining about her precious garden.'

Harlan joined Natalie in blocking the door. 'No,' he said to the room. 'Think about it. Our dues keep rising, but the common areas keep deteriorating, even though Paige insists all our houses, yards, and even mailboxes look perfect. But if the board needs to write a check – to fix the brick path around the pond, to repair the clubhouse gutters, or even to spread mulch under the play structure – nothing happens.'

'Exactly,' said Natalie, over mounting murmurs. 'Detective Ford, find out where our money went, and you'll find Jim's murderer.'

'The Tranquil Oaks records are confidential and password-protected,' said Paige. 'I won't let you pry into our business.' Natalie worried the records would vanish before a search warrant was issued.

'But I will,' said Tori, raising her hand. 'I have access as treasurer.'

'How about now?' said the detective, striding toward the back door and grasping Paige's arm. 'You'd better come along too.' Natalie and Harlan stepped aside, Detective Ford exited with Paige and Tori, and the door banged shut behind them.

During the stunned split second before cacophony engulfed the room, Natalie heard a soft 'I need a brownie' as Sloane made a beeline toward the dessert table.

&a.

The next week, while news of Paige's arrest on first-degree murder and grand larceny charges consumed Tranquil Oaks, Natalie focused elsewhere. At long last, she found an ideal spot for a new bakery, and because her co-owner at Breaktime Coffee offered to buy-out her half-interest, she could just about afford it. The catch: The new location was near the University of Maryland, on the opposite side of Washington, D.C. and halfway around the Capital Beltway from her northern Virginia neighborhood. Natalie knew the distance was a deal-breaker.

'The commute would be exhausting,' she told Harlan over dinner, 'especially with the longer hours I'd work.' She hung her head and stared at her nearly full plate of tomato-basil penne. 'I'd spend ninety minutes in traffic, or even longer on Metro, each way.'

'So, you can't open a bakery there as long as we live here,' Harlan said.

'Right.' Natalie prodded her fork. 'And I know you don't want to move.'

'I've reconsidered.' Harlan smiled and his eyes sparkled. 'I agree it's time for a fresh start.'

Natalie leapt to her feet, laughed, and wrapped her husband in a tight hug. She was prepared for hard work ahead, but now at least one decision was easy: 'A Fresh Start' was the perfect name for her new bakery.

BIO:

DK Snyder is a writer and a lawyer. Her flash fiction appears in online magazines including *Shotgun Honey* and *Cease, Cows*, and her short fiction is forthcoming in *Ellery Queen's Mystery Magazine*. She lives in Virginia with her husband, whom she thanks for assistance with the recipe included in *Lemons and Lies*.

RECIPE

Natalie's Lemon-Rosemary Scones

Ingredients
2 ¼ cups all-purpose flour
½ cup sugar
1 tablespoon baking powder
½ teaspoon salt
Zest and juice from 1 lemon (about 2 tablespoons juice)
1 tablespoon chopped fresh rosemary, plus extra leaves for decoration
1 ½ sticks (¾ cup) unsalted butter, cold
2/3 cup sour cream
Decorating sugar

Method
Preheat oven to 375°F (190°C).
Sift together flour, sugar, baking powder and salt. Add lemon zest and chopped rosemary; stir to combine.
Cut butter into the flour mixture with a pastry cutter until the pieces are pea sized. Add sour cream and lemon juice. Stir gently until a smooth dough forms.

Turn dough onto a floured surface. Roll into a rectangle ½ - ¾ inches thick, approximately 8 x 11 inches. Cut into 6 rectangles, then cut each rectangle diagonally to form 12 triangles. Place triangles on a parchment-lined cookie sheet. Press a single full rosemary leaf onto the top of each triangle. Sprinkle with decorating sugar. If the dough has warmed up too much, cool in freezer for about 10 minutes.

Bake in oven for 24-28 minutes, until golden brown. Remove and allow to cool before eating.

Chapter Eleven

MEATBALL MURDER

Paula Barr

Dana started a new career making international meatballs for her food truck. But when a community theater star player dies after eating one of her meatball subs, Dana becomes the number one suspect. She needs to find the real killer before Maplewood's biased detective tosses her in the clink.

Dana Anderson tapped her fingernails on the counter in her Magnificent Meatballs food truck as her competitor continued to rant.

'Excuse me, but you're holding up my customers,' Dana said between gritted teeth. If she were twenty years younger, she'd pour a jug of iced tea over Tabitha Creak's head. Sadly, society expected more self-control from a forty-two-year-old. 'Can we discuss this later?'

The young blonde stood on tiptoe and leaned in closer as if Dana hadn't heard her. 'If people want Italian food, they should come to my pasta truck. You'd better stop stealing my customers, or else.' Tabitha said, shaking her fist.

Dana wasn't about to let Tabitha ruin things. Her first day at the Maplewood Summer Festival had already earned her as much revenue as in her first month on the streets. 'Italy doesn't have a monopoly on meatballs,' Dana spat, as she pointed to the international menu hanging next to the counter. 'I'm not taking any of your business.'

'I'm here to stay, Tabitha.' Dana crossed her arms and glared. 'If you're so worried about losing business, how about you go back to your spaghetti truck and stop wasting both our time.' She looked past Tabitha.

'Next.'

'I'll have Kofta Kababs,' said a customer as he jostled past Tabitha to the counter.

Tabitha's face turned three shades of indignation. 'You'll regret ever coming to this town,' she snarled. As she whipped around, her ponytail knocked the napkin holder off the shelf. *Too bad that ponytail didn't land in a bowl of spicy mustard.*

Dana smiled as she put three skewers of meatballs on a plate. Her mouth watered at the delicious aroma of onions, mint and other spices in the grilled beef and rice mixture.

'Enjoy,' she said as she handed the plate to the customer.

Dana worked diligently through the next forty-five minutes of non-stop orders before she finally managed to eke out a break.

Dana closed the window on the truck and sat in the grass nearby to relax and people watch. She gazed at Tabitha's food truck, parked on the outskirts, away from the activities.

She's just angry that she's farther away from the action. But that's no reason to take it out on me.

'Who upset your apple cart? Your face looks like a thundercloud.' A husky voice pulled Dana from her stewing.

She smiled at the tall lumberjack of a man walking toward her. His bare forearms reminded Dana of Popeye the Sailor Man, and the clingy shirt showed off his six-pack. Dana felt her heart skip when he smiled.

'Hey there, Timothy. Eh, I just let Tabitha get under my skin. Are you enjoying the festival?'

'Yeah, it's even bigger than last year. Just thought I'd stop by and see if you wanted to take a walk.'

'Sure, I've got a little time.' They strolled past the games and reached over a fence to pet a trio of goats.

'How do you like Connecticut?'

'I'm still unpacking, but my uncle's house is starting to feel more like home. I wish I'd spent more time with him.' Dana's eyes welled up. 'I was really surprised when his lawyer called me about the will. Uncle Joe is the reason I was able to start my meatball truck.'

'Yeah, Joe was a great guy. He had one heck of a voice – people came to the plays mostly to hear him sing. In fact, he's the reason I got involved with the theater group.'

'I had no idea. Are you an actor, too?'

'No way. I just work on the set and make sure nothing falls down,' Timothy said with a laugh that revealed dimples on each cheek. Dana felt a tingle that she tried to ignore.

'I haven't been to a play in forever.'

'There's often more drama behind the scenes than on the stage.' Timothy winked. 'Oh, the stories I could tell you.'

The sudden clapping from the crowd signified the end of the

band's set. 'I'd love to hear them, but right now I'd better get back to the truck.'

After serving several customers, Dana was amused to see a man at the counter who was dressed in a white shirt with a huge ruff collar, brocade vest, long maroon coat, tan breeches, and black boots that came to his knees. The man greeted her with a theatrical bow.

'Good morning, m'lady. Byron Slyk here. A pleasure to make your acquaintance. How be you on this fine day?'

'Fine, thank you,' she replied, fighting an urge to roll her eyes. 'Is there a play today?

'Whatever do you mean?'

'The way you're dressed...oh never mind. What can I get you?'

Byron looked over the menu. 'Pray tell, could you explain the choices?'

'My meatballs come from around the world. Kofta Kebabs are Persian, Keftedes are Greek, Köttbullar are Swedish. The Spanish meatballs are from Spain, of course, but don't order them if you are allergic to almonds.'

'My mouth be watering at the thought. I'll try the Spanish meatballs and my wife will have the kebabs.' He broke character and hollered, 'Patricia. Come.'

'She's your wife, not your dog.' Maplewood Detective Sam Harrey stomped across the grass and into Byron's personal space. 'Have some respect.'

A painfully thin woman with streaks of grey in her hair and a face carved from despair joined Byron and glanced at the detective. 'It's okay, Sam,' she said quietly.

Dana handed the plates to Byron, who shoved them into his wife's hands. 'Carry these.' He bowed again to Dana, then turned and sauntered off. The woman shot the detective a worried look that Dana felt lingered a little too long. Harrey gave her a slight nod, and Patricia shuffled after her husband, a plate in each hand.

'What a piece of work,' Dana muttered.

'Hey. We don't take kindly to outsiders talking bad about our residents,' the detective snapped at her.

Dana's mouth dropped open. 'Wow. Why are you sticking up for that guy? You were just yelling at him. And for the record, I live here, too.'

'As far as I'm concerned, you're still a stranger. So, be careful what you say about us Maplewoodians.' Detective Harrey spun on his heels and followed Patricia at a distance.

Yikes.

Dana watched as Byron walked over to Tabitha's truck. He spoke briefly with the woman and left with a drink and another plate.

Are my portions not big enough? Well...at least Tabitha can't say that I'm stealing her customers now.

A slender man with a blonde bowl cut and a goatee was next in line. 'That guy you were talking to is a real creep. He ought to be thankful that woman stays with him because no one else would.'

He introduced himself as Roger Davis and ordered Swedish meatballs.

'What's up with that guy and the costume?' Dana chuckled.

'Our theater group did a scene this morning. The rest of us changed clothes, but he wants everyone to know he's a 'star thespian." Roger snorted. 'He's a hack. Rumor is, he's got something on the director, and that's why he always gets the lead.'

'Why doesn't anyone talk to the director?' Dana asked as she handed him his food.

'Oh, we have, but he just tells us Byron did the best in the audition. Every single time.' Roger scowled and walked off grumbling.

Not long after, Dana regretted not visiting the porta potty during her stroll with Timothy. *Drat. Now I have to walk all the way across the fairgrounds.* She closed up again and hurried to the parking lot to the portable restrooms.

Dana pulled open the door to find Byron, slumped against the toilet, his eyes wide open and opaque. White foam and vomit had spilled out of his mouth and onto the white ruff. A paper plate and two meatballs lay next to his body.

'Help, somebody help.' Dana screamed repeatedly.

She heard running behind her but couldn't take her eyes off Byron.

'Get away from him.' Detective Harrey barked. He pulled Dana back and spoke to the crowd who had gathered. 'All of you, go back to the festival. Now.'

Dana turned to leave, but Harrey grabbed the back of her shirt. 'Not you.'

He took a quick look at Byron and radioed dispatch. 'Call the coroner and tell him to get to the fairgrounds pronto.'

The detective snapped on a pair of gloves, then kneeled down for a closer look. He scowled at Dana. 'Do you know anything about this?'

'Of course not. I just found him like that.'

'He hasn't been dead long.' Harrey leaned closer to Byron's face.

'Almonds. Smells like cyanide,' he muttered, then stated, 'This man's been poisoned.'

He pointed at the plate on the ground, and the words 'Magnificent Meatballs' printed on it in bright red letters. 'And it looks like he's been eating your meatballs.'

'Well, I certainly didn't poison him.'

Harrey picked up one of the meatballs from the ground and sniffed it. 'Aha. This smells like almonds as well.'

'That's because I use almond sauce on my Spanish meatballs,' Dana retorted. 'Look, Detective, I don't do made-to-order meatballs, I make them in batches. I can't even count how many of these I've sold today. If they were poisoned, you'd have a lot more dead bodies.'

'Well, ma'am, I need you to come down to the station to answer some questions.' Harrey pulled out a pair of handcuffs.

'You've got to be kidding.'

Harrey cuffed her and took her to the patrol car. At the police station, he led Dana into a small room, cuffed her to the table, and grilled her.

'This is insane,' she exclaimed. 'You don't even know the cause of death yet. And even if it was poison, there's no poison in my meatballs.'

Harrey leaned closer. 'Listen, lady. I've got a dead guy who's been eating your meatballs. We haven't had a murder in this town in decades. Then you move in and suddenly, there's a body. Why wouldn't I be suspicious?'

'Detective, I'd never seen the man until he came to my truck today. I've already met multiple people who weren't fans of his. Besides, you act like my meatballs are all he ate, but you saw him get another plate of food from the spaghetti truck. Unless you have enough evidence to charge me, this interrogation is over. I'm leaving.'

'I can hold you up to seventy-two hours without charging you.'

'You're going to waste seventy-two hours holding me without even looking into other suspects? You're going to look so dumb when you find out there's no poison in my meatballs.' Dana shook her head in exasperation.

Harrey mumbled under his breath. 'Fine, you can go. But I'm watching you. Don't think you're in the clear.'

'I'm not the only food truck who served him. Why didn't you arrest Tabitha?'

'Tabitha grew up here. I trust the people of this town. It's strangers that I don't trust.'

Dana stormed out of the room and found Timothy waiting in the lobby.

'I'm so glad to see you,' he said. 'What was Harrey thinking?' He followed Dana out the door and gestured for her to get into his truck.

'He's thinking that I poisoned Byron with my meatballs. He

let me go for now, but if that autopsy shows there really was poison in the meat, Harrey will lock me up faster than I can pan fry a Keftedes.'

'I'm sure the coroner's report will clear you,' Timothy said, starting the truck.

'Heck, no. I'm not waiting around for that detective to pin this murder on me. I'm going to find the real killer before I end up behind bars.'

'How are you going to do that? You're not Jessica Fletcher or Miss Marple.'

'I don't know. I guess I'll just start asking questions and go from there.'

'I'm not sure that's a good idea,' Timothy chided.

'I'm not asking for your opinion. Harrey's clearly got it out for me, so I can't afford to sit around and wait for him to come back with handcuffs.'

Timothy glanced at Dana as he parked at the fairgrounds. 'Okay, but I'm going to help. There's a killer out there, and I don't want you to be his next victim.'

'Thanks. I can use your help. I guess I'm done selling for the day.'

As she closed up the food truck, Dana thought about potential suspects. 'There's me and Tabitha. Roger didn't like him. Is there anyone else who might have a grudge against Byron?'

'Me.'

'You? Why?'

'Byron was a scumbag. I hated the way he behaved toward the actresses – and, even worse, the way he treated his wife. If anyone saw the blowout we had yesterday, I'm sure I look mighty suspicious.'

Dana looked at Timothy for a long moment, waiting for him to say the thing he'd left unsaid. Finally, she spoke: 'Are you going to make me ask?'

'Of course, I didn't kill the guy. Geeze.' Timothy turned his head away, but not before Dana could see the hurt in his eyes.

'I'm sorry. I know you couldn't kill someone any more than I could. But somebody wanted Byron dead – what about his wife?'

'That poor woman gave up her family, her friends, and her freedom when she married that louse. I wouldn't blame her if she killed him.'

'Well, the spouse is always the first suspect, but not always the best.' Dana noted. 'Anyone else?'

'I agree that Roger could be a suspect. I heard a rumor that a director from the state theater company is planning to be at our next play. Byron bragged that this would be his big break. Maybe Roger wanted that opportunity for himself.'

'Well, let's go find him,' Dana said, peering at the crowd.

They found Roger playing in the croquet tournament. The two approached the actor when he finished his turn.

'Isn't it awful about Byron?'

'Good riddance, I'd say. Couldn't have happened to a better guy. Now maybe a real actor will have a chance for the lead.'

'When's the last time you saw him?' Dana tried to sound innocuous, but Roger stiffened.

'Why? Are you trying to imply I had something to do with his death?'

'No, of course not. I was just curious.'

'I wouldn't have any idea what happened to Byron.' Roger spun on his heel and stomped back to the game.

'You know him. What do you think?' Dana asked.

Timothy shrugged. 'He seems pretty happy that Byron's dead. I'd keep him on your list.' A woman waved from a nearby food truck.

'I need to talk to Phyliss. Can you wait for me here?' Dana pointed to a bench before walking over to the pastry truck.

Phyllis Todd, Uncle Joe's former sweetheart, had taken Dana under her wing after Joe died. She greeted Dana with a smile. 'Hello, my dear. You have to try my new Danish.'

Dana sunk her teeth into the lemon-filled pastry and felt her taste buds dance.

'You have outdone yourself, Phyllis.'

'Thank you, sweetie. Did you hear about Byron?'

'I'm the one who found him.'

'That must have been ghastly,' Phyllis gasped.

'Especially because now Detective Harrey thinks I'm the one who did it.'

'Maybe that doggone Sam Harrey should be looking at his own self,' Phyllis sputtered. 'He's been moony over Patricia Slyk since they were kids. If I didn't know better, I'd think he might have tried to get rid of Byron.'

Aha. I knew there was something to that look.

'He sure seemed protective of Patricia at my truck. If he killed Byron, that would explain why he is determined to pin the murder on me. Case solved and he goes free.'

Phyllis shook her head. 'I was just being catty. There's no way Harrey would hurt anyone. He lives by the law, and I'd bet my life he's innocent.'

'Well, he sure has it in for me. He thinks I killed Byron with poisoned meatballs.'

'Oh, for heaven's sake. I mean, your meatballs are to die for— but that's absurd. You'd never poison anyone. But Harrey doesn't trust newcomers until he knows more about them. He's fiercely protective of this town and the people in it. To a fault, if you ask me.'

'If it turns out there really was poison in the meatballs, someone had to have put it there after Byron left my truck.' Dana theorized. 'You know, Roger Davis wasn't a fan. Do you know anything about him?'

'Oh, Roger and Byron hated each other.' Phyllis nodded. 'Roger's ambitious and has always been jealous that Byron got the lead in every play. Honestly, he's better suited as a leading man, and Byron knew it. I don't know how Roger could get close enough to administer poison, though. They avoided each other like the plague when they weren't on stage.'

'One person who could get close to Byron was his wife,' Dana suggested. 'From what I hear, he was emotionally abusive.'

'Well, she's another one whose motive I could understand. Byron treated her like a servant.' Phyllis paused. 'If Patricia did kill her husband, it's going to be hard for Detective Harrey to arrest her. But you should probably narrow down the other suspects before accusing a lawman and a grieving widow.'

'I don't know who else could have done it.' Dana sighed.

'Maybe it's someone you aren't even considering. But be careful. Nosing around might make the killer nervous enough to come after you,' Phyllis said, placing her hand on Dana's.

'I'll be careful. I promise,' Dana replied. 'But I need to find out more about Roger. Do you know anyone I could talk to about him?'

'I'd try the theater. He spends most of his time there.'

Dana returned to Timothy at the bench. 'Hey, could you show me where the theater is? Maybe someone there might know something.'

The theater was in an old barn across from the fairgrounds. As they stepped inside, Dana picked up the faint smell of hay and livestock, the only sign of the building's former use. Timothy took her backstage, where the crew was busy with scenery and props.

'This is Lydia,' Timothy said, introducing her to a woman who was sorting a rackful of clothes. 'She's in charge of costumes for every play.'

'Every play? That must keep you busy.'

'It sure does. I can always use more help,' Lydia said, with an exaggerated wink.

The three made small talk about past plays until Dana found an opening to ask about Roger. 'I met him earlier today. He was complaining that Byron is always the leading man in your plays. He sure wasn't happy about that.'

'Not happy? More like crazy jealous,' Lydia snorted. 'I can't say as I blame him. Roger would have been a better leading man in many of our plays.'

'Was he angry enough that he would try to hurt Byron?'

Lydia thought for a moment before she replied. 'I can't say for certain. But I wouldn't be surprised if Roger snapped. He could be a star, but Byron always gets the roles, so he never gets his chance to shine.'

'Do you know Patricia?'

'Not very well. Byron didn't let anyone get close to her,' Lydia said with a frown. 'He was a real creep. Nobody understands why he keeps getting cast in the best parts.'

'I heard Byron had something over the director. Maybe a little blackmail?'

'I wouldn't put it past him,' Lydia said. 'Byron was a narcissist, and most people couldn't stand him.'

'I know the type,' Dana replied. 'I was married to one.'

'You should talk to Catherine. She's helping me with accessories.' Lydia pointed to an older woman who was sorting through jewelry. 'She did the happy dance when we heard Byron was dead. Catherine is the only person I know who spent time with Patricia.'

Dana raised an eyebrow and looked at Timothy. They thanked Lydia, then Dana introduced herself to Catherine.

'Poor Patricia,' Dana said as she sidled up next to the woman. 'What a shock to find your husband murdered. I can't imagine how she must be feeling.'

'I imagine she's home bawling her eyes out. But to be honest, if it were me, I'd be crying tears of joy. That man was a monster,' Catherine spewed. 'His killer deserves a medal. I wish I'd had the guts to do it myself.'

'Could Particia have done it? She wouldn't be the first abused wife to snap.'

'Oh, lord, no.' Catherine shook her head emphatically. 'That woman is the sweetest person you'd ever want to meet. Never complains. Wouldn't harm a flea.'

'Can you think of anyone who would want him dead?'

Catherine started naming names and counting them with her fingers until she reached ten. 'I'd keep going but I'd have to take off my shoes,' she chuckled.

Dana and Timothy continued questioning the crew, before dropping onto a worn couch.

'I feel so hopeless,' Dana complained. 'People didn't like Byron, but I'm no closer to figuring out who might have done the deed. Let's head back to the fairgrounds.'

'Maybe someone in the food court saw something,' Timothy suggested.

They were walking down the side of the barn when Dana stopped short.

'Timothy, did you hear that?' she whispered.

'Hear what?'

'I just heard someone say Byron's name.' She motioned for him to follow her. They crept toward the back of the barn, straining to hear. With backs against the wall, they eased toward the end of the building.

'Are you sure no one saw you walk away from the porta potty?'

Tabitha.

'Well, I didn't think so. But this woman's nosing around and now I'm not sure,' Roger's frenzied voice replied.

'You better not have screwed this up.'

'Me screw this up.? If you'd put enough poison in his smoothie, we'd be in the clear. Why'd you use yew leaves instead of rat poison like we planned?'

'Keep your voice down,' Tabitha scolded. 'I needed something that took longer than ten minutes to kick in, or else he would have dropped dead next to my truck.'

'This is so much messier than it was supposed to be,' Roger whined.

'We just need to stay calm. The cops suspect the meatball

vendor. So, if we keep our heads down, no one should even look our way.'

'Go call the cops,' Dana whispered to Timothy. 'I'll keep an eye on them.'

He nodded and slipped away so the killers wouldn't hear the call. Dana listened as the couple continued to bicker, but a low buzzing behind her broke her concentration. She looked back to see a swarm of yellow jackets zooming out of a hive next to where Timothy had been standing.

'Yikes.' Dana yelled as she instinctively jumped back from the barn.

The conversation stopped.

'Who's there?' Tabitha turned and locked eyes with Dana. Her face grew cold, and she screamed: 'YOU. How much did you hear?'

Roger ran up and grabbed Dana. 'Oh, this is just great. Now what are we gonna do?'

'We're going to have to get rid of her.'

Dana struggled to get loose. 'You killed Byron. I won't let you get away with that.'

She drew her leg back and kicked Roger in the shin as hard as she could. The moment his grip weakened, she pulled away and took off. But Tabitha followed, hot on her heels, and tackled Dana to the ground.

'Help,' Dana yelled as she struggled to get up. Tabitha reached her arm around Dana's neck and started to squeeze.

Dana pried at the young woman's arm, managing to squeeze one hand under the arm to keep Tabitha from locking in the chokehold. Then she reached back with the other and clawed at Tabitha's face, gouging one of her eyes.

Suddenly, Dana felt Tabitha being ripped from her back. She turned to see Timothy tossing the woman to the ground before rounding on Roger.

The thespian took one look at Timothy and took off running.

'Go get him,' Dana yelled. She lunged at Tabitha and rolled on top of her, pinning the other woman to the ground.

Tabitha squirmed beneath her, tears streaming from the injured eye.

'Give up,' Dana commanded.

Instead, Tabitha threw her head forward in a vicious head butt. Dana barely managed to dodge by throwing herself to the side. Tabitha took advantage of this opening to buck Dana off and reclaim the top position. Once there, she sank an elbow into the other woman's breast. Dana screamed and the pain stunned her for a second, giving her opponent time to settle onto her chest. Tabitha wrapped her hands around Dana's neck.

Dana struggled to breathe as her opponent's hands tightened. She tried to reach Tabitha's face again, but the woman blocked her this time and squeezed harder. Dana's vision started to narrow, and she frantically flailed her hands, seeking anything to use as a weapon.

Finally, her fingers grazed a stick just beyond her grasp. Summoning the little strength she had left, Dana bucked under her assailant until she wriggled close enough to pick up the limb. Just before everything went dark, she swung with all her might and connected with Tabitha's head.

CRACK.

Tabitha fell to the ground, and Dana twisted out from under her, coughing and gasping for air. When her vision fully returned, she saw Tabitha lying unconscious.

'I'd feel a lot sorrier for you if you hadn't just tried to kill me, you witch,' Dana croaked.

Heavy footsteps approached as Timothy appeared carrying an unconscious Roger. 'The cops should be here any minute. Are you okay?'

'Yeah. How about you?'

'Yeah, not a scratch,' he said with a smirk. 'I'd love to say I subdued him with my manly strength, but the truth is, he ran into a low-hanging branch.'

Moments later, Detective Harrey came running over from the festival grounds, gun drawn. He holstered it when he saw the unconscious pair. 'What happened here?'

'They killed Byron,' Dana explained. 'And she tried to kill me.'

Tabitha moaned and opened her eyes as Harrey knelt down to handcuff her before turning his attention to Roger. He and Timothy brought the culprits to the patrol car that was pulling into the parking lot.

Harrey nodded at Dana. 'I'm still keeping an eye on you, outsider.'

Dana laughed. 'Is that your way of saying thanks for catching the killers?'

Harrey gave a lopsided grin as he loaded the criminals into the car.

A paramedic ran up the drive. 'I'm on duty at the fairgrounds, and I got a call to head over here.'

Harrey jerked a thumb toward Dana. 'You need to check them out.' He jumped in the passenger side of the patrol car and called out before they left, 'You two, come to the station when the medic clears you. I need to ask you some questions.'

The paramedic examined Dana, who only had bumps and bruises. She and Timothy walked to his truck and drove to the police station.

'How are you really doing?' Timothy asked as he drove.

'I'm still a little shaken, but mostly I am relieved that it's all over.'

They waited in the lobby for nearly two hours before Harrey came out and sat with them. 'You'll be happy to know we got a full confession.'

'Why did they do it?' Dana asked. 'Was it really worth killing someone over a role in the community theater?'

'They thought so. Roger was convinced he had a shot at working his way into a professional theater company if he got the chance to prove himself. That was never going to happen as long as Byron kept getting the limelight.'

'We heard a rumor that a big shot director was coming to the next play,' Timothy said.

'Well, I don't know whether that was true, but Roger believed it. He was sure that the director would be interested in recruiting him if Roger was the leading man. And he got it in his head that the only way to keep Bryon from stealing that chance was to kill the man.'

'Tabitha said something about poisoning him with yew. What was that about?'

The detective shrugged. 'Yeah, that's a new one for me. Apparently, everything on the yew tree is poisonous but the berries. There's plenty of the trees around here, so it was just a matter of Tabitha gathering leaves and putting them in a blender. The fruits and vegetables in the smoothie hid the taste. Once Byron started getting sick, he headed to the porta potty.'

'It sounded like they were accusing each other of messing things up, but Byron died. Why did they think something went wrong,' Dana asked.

'Roger was afraid Byron would vomit up the poison, so he strangled him and left him next to the toilet.'

'So, not my meatballs after all. I *told* you that's not what killed him.' Dana crossed her arms and gave Harrey a smug look.

'Yeah, well, if you hadn't put almonds in the sauce, I might not have jumped to that conclusion,' Harrey growled. 'Look, I just need to get your statements, and you're free to go.'

'One more thing. Why did Tabitha get involved in this?'

'She and Roger were having an affair. Turns out she's in the middle of a divorce and Bryon was blackmailing her. He had compromising photos of the couple and was threatening to show her husband. Tabitha believed if her husband caught wind of the affair, he would take her to the cleaners in the divorce.'

'Byron wasn't a nice guy, but he didn't deserve this,' Timothy said.

'You're lucky to be alive,' Harrey chided. 'You shouldn't have nosed around,'

'So you could pin the murder on me?' Dana protested. 'No way.'

Harrey shook his head and stood up. 'Come on, Timothy, let's get your statement first.'

The detective walked to the lobby door and waved Timothy in. Before closing the door behind them, Harrey turned to smile at Dana. 'Welcome to Maplewood, meatball lady.'

BIO:

Paula is a member of Sisters in Crime and a board member of its Desert Sleuths chapter in Phoenix, Arizona. In addition to writing cozy mysteries, she is finishing a braided memoir about the death penalty. When she is not at her computer, Paula loves reading, traveling, and hiking with her dog, Meghan.

RECIPE

Spanish Meatballs

There are several ways to make Spanish meatballs, but I usually make mine with tomato sauce. Using almond sauce in the story tied better into Dana's plight. If you are allergic to or don't like almonds, substitute your favorite tomato sauce.

Ingredients
1 pound ground pork
½ pound ground beef
2 eggs
2/3 cup breadcrumbs (I use Italian)

¼ cup chopped onion
2 cloves minced garlic
1 tsp. ground black pepper
½ tsp. nutmeg
1 tsp. paprika
2 tbsp. fresh parsley
Olive oil for frying
Flour to coat meatballs

Optional
Salt to taste (1-2 tsps.) if desired

Almond Sauce
2/3 cup white wine
1 pinch saffron
¼ cup olive oil
3 garlic cloves
4 slices white bread (remove crusts and cut into quarters)
2/3 cup chicken broth
½ cup raw almonds

Method
Combine meat, eggs, garlic, parsley, salt, pepper, and breadcrumbs into a bowl. Add more breadcrumbs if needed to make balls. Place plastic wrap on top of the meat and put the bowl in the refrigerator for a few hours (can stay overnight). Roll chilled meat into medium-sized balls, then roll in flour. Fry in olive oil until the meatballs are brown on all sides. Drain on paper towels. Meatballs should be pink on the inside, as they will cook more in the sauce.

Sauce
In a separate pan, pour saffron into the white wine, then prepare the sauce.
Sauté garlic cloves in olive oil over medium heat until golden brown. Remove from oil and put in food processor or blender.
Fry raw almonds in the same oil until they start to turn a golden color. Do not let them burn. Add them to the garlic.
Fry the bread slices in the same oil on high heat to make croutons. Add to the other ingredients when crisp.
Add chicken stock and the infused wine to the food processor/blender and blend until smooth, about 1 minute.

Cooking
Place meatballs in large frying pan and add sauce. Cook over *very low* heat for 20 minutes. Add water if sauce gets too thick.
Taste, then add salt and pepper to your preferences.

Serving suggestions
Serve with rice or potatoes and a salad (or vegetables) for a main course.

ACKNOWLEDGMENTS

Thank you to all those who continue to buy my books and the books of every author in this anthology. Without you, the readers, we would be nothing.

Thanks also go to all the members of History Writers and City Writers who are there to bounce ideas and advise as necessary.

Final thanks to my writing buddies, Sheena Macleod, Susan McVey (Marti M. McNair) and Pauline Tait. We spend many hours discussing all things writing and publishing. It's amazing how many hours can pass in this way.

ALSO BY WENDY H. JONES

In this series

A Right Cozy Christmas Crime

Coming Soon

A Right Cozy Historical Crime

www.ingramcontent.com/pod-product-compliance
Lightning Source LLC
Chambersburg PA
CBHW031957180726
48283CB00008B/2465